DEDICATION

When I began *The Divided Twin*, I always knew the one person I was writing to—my oldest son, Austin Thomas.

"Austin, my Austin" is what my mom, your grandma, called you. Of all her grandchildren, you reminded her most of my father. You have his wonderfully round, Charlie Brown–shaped head and contagious smile, and when you laugh, it brightens the room. When you were little, you climbed—everything. You were fearless. If I turned around, you'd be on the backyard fence or on the highest rung of the jungle gym. What I didn't realize was just how far you'd climb. From studying abroad to earning a double major in college, there is no height too high.

As the firstborn twin, if only by a minute, you have always taken charge and worn the mantle of responsibility for your brothers and sister proudly. You are the protector, the overachiever, and one who leads with his heart. You fearlessly approach life with drive, compassion, and strength with an unending spirit that never gives up.

Austin, you are my hero.

And I couldn't have written this book without you. When I was diagnosed with breast cancer, you were the child who tried to make my life easier. My sweet son, from the depths of my heart—thank you.

Parts of the letter you wrote me when I was diagnosed are included in this book. How could I ever write anything better or more heartfelt?

You would make any parent proud. I'm the lucky one who gets that honor. And being your mom is the greatest gift I've ever been given.

Keep climbing.

Austin, my Austin, I will love you forever and ever.

-Ma

Everyone has a voice in their head – mine is just a little louder.

DEDICATION

Mr. Mike Allred

When in the process of creating *The Divided Twin*, I often had to reflect on the emotional and physical traumas that I had experienced with my battle of mental illness. Throughout my life, I have had many people help me through these issues, but someone who has remained etched in my mind was my 5th grade teacher in Etna, Wyoming— Mr. Mike Allred.

When I was in his class, he taught me many things that have stuck with me throughout my life, but the most prominent of these lessons was that everything was going to be okay. At the time that I was in his class, I had already been experiencing many symptoms of my illness, and as a teacher, he picked up on these tendencies almost immediately.

I will never forget the words he told me as I was taking a math test during his class. He would notice that whenever I was in a stressful situation, I would cough every couple of seconds. During this test, I was coughing quite frequently, and he came over to my desk, put his hand on my shoulder, and whispered in my ear, "You are okay, and I promise you that there is nothing to fear in my class." Those simple words of encouragement have carried quite a weight throughout my life, and I will never forget the man who inspired me to get through the day and remember that everything is okay.

This book is an escape for all that I have been through with mental illness. However, it remains a work of fiction. Writing allows me to share the emotions of mental illness. The actions that these characters take are not from personal experience; many of the emotions, though, are.

I dedicate *The Divided Twin* in its entirety to a man who helped me feel safe through troubling times. Thank you, Mr. Allred.

-Kyle Thomas

#

A note to our readers

While there are similarities to our journey through mental illness, this book is a work of fiction. In writing *The Divided Twin*, Kyle and I thought, *What if...?* and let our imaginations run free. The gift of fiction is that it allows the what-ifs in life to live, if even for a moment in time.

If you struggle with depression or another mental illness, you're not alone. Please reach out to someone. Help can be found at the National Institute of Mental Health (NIMH) or by calling their help line: **866-415-8051**

CHAPTER 1

DAVID AND ME

A photo of three girls wearing nothing more than silver ski jackets, furry boots, and smiles while huddled beside me in an ice bar surfaced on my laptop.

I leaned forward, and the tip of my baseball cap tapped the touch screen, bringing the image into greater focus. A blonde, a brunette, and a redhead—the trifecta of hot—cleaved to me for warmth like an alcoholic clung to their bottle. *Damn, I looked good.* Not that I should be surprised. David always looked out for me. He was the only one who told me that, with my beard and messy hair, my style was on point. *Hell yeah.*

I skimmed the comments on my Instagram page and grinned.

#pimp
Just hoes and tricks, man.
#icebarbitches

I scanned the other pics on my page, each one showing me with a different girl in a different city. I kept my account private from prying eyes that wouldn't understand—like my mom. If she knew what I did with her tuition checks, she'd lose her shit. But let's get real: when I followed David's suggestions, I was the life of the party. Besides, he wouldn't have my ear so much if my family wasn't so pathetic.

I cracked my neck, and a loud pop followed. My health teacher in high school always told me that cracking my neck or any joint was bad for my body, but fuck that; it relieved pressure.

"I mean, why wouldn't you do something that feels good?"

Agreed.

I opened a Word document, cracked my knuckles, and let David direct my thoughts.

A Killer's Journal

This journal will comprise the thoughts, feelings, and actions taken by an individual who has had killer tendencies. The individual has never killed or seriously harmed anyone before but has the natural instinct to do so. This journal is meant to be left anonymous and to be used for research purposes only.

I was about to continue when the tip of her tail brushed

my elbow.

"Bonita." I stroked her neck and down the length of her muscular body. Her almond-shaped eyes closed and purring ensued. "Yeah, yeah, I know."

Her long legs lingered along the edge of my chair, and then with one graceful hop, she situated herself on my desk beside my laptop.

"Bonita, I have work to do."

When her large ears pointed up and her strikingly blue eyes peered at me from behind the chocolate mask that covered her face, I was putty in her paws.

"That's the only reason I took you home. I didn't even know what a Siamese cat was." But Bonita reminded me of someone I once knew. What I didn't expect was that a cat craved more attention and affection than my identical twin brother, which I didn't think was humanly possible.

"Okay, okay, let me get back to work."

The beauty about Bonita was that she didn't speak.

"First time an animal opens their jaw and starts to talk, they're as good as gone."

Agreed.

I returned my attention to the screen and resumed typing.

I feel like most people don't remember the moment or times of insanity. I, however, recall every excruciating minute and feeling of those times of loss of sanity and judgment.

It all started with the abuse of my

family. I've discovered through all my college readings that many theorists will tell you—or rather theorize—that tracing the subject's history to their past will find the answer to a majority of mental health issues. Abuse, whether mental, physical, or sexual, often leads to some sort of problem in the future.

I've never been sexually abused, but I have been physically abused and witnessed physical abuse, which theorists believe leads to mental abuse as well. I don't remember all of the times my dad hurt my mom, but I do remember one certain instance.

Bonita purred and her tail swayed, which sent fur in the air that I knew would instantly stick to my black shirt. I was forever picking Bonita hair off my clothes. I brushed my sleeve.

"Stupid fucking cat."

And just as quickly as Bonita had appeared, she left.

I returned my focus to my computer entry.

My brother and I were in our rooms listening to the lovely night conversations of our parents. It was typical chatter with yelling, screaming, and the occasional punches. After a little while, we went to investigate to make sure Dad hadn't gone too far. We went downstairs after hearing Mom and Dad in their room having a "discussion." We patiently waited for the chatter to die down, but all we could hear was the increase in our father's voice. Shortly afterward, our pregnant mother came out of the room with our father close behind. While my mom made her way down the stairs, our father came behind her and gave her a rather sturdy push, which sent my pregnant mom tumbling down the staircase.

But it wasn't like a light fall. My mom's pregnant belly made her top heavy, so she flipped head over heels a few times before she caught her balance—if she really ever did. My brother got hit by my dad for interfering and telling my old man to stop, and I was forced to watch. I remember locking eyes with my mom and realizing how hopeless our lives were as she bled from her lower body.

It wasn't like a gush of blood, but my mom held her stomach as if she could stop the slow trickle of blood that stained the carpet and her hands. No matter how much she tried to save the life seeping out of her, *she couldn't.*

I ran to the neighbor's house to get help, but as I rang the doorbell and beat my knuckles against the door, no one answered. No one came. Except my father. He picked me up like a sack of trash he had forgotten and took me home.

I remember that I was not full of fear during those moments but rather curiosity of what it would feel like to inflict pain on others. Was it joyful, fun even? I believe I was five at the time when these questions bothered my every waking moment and I wanted to explore this understanding.

I leaned back until I teetered on the hind legs of the chair and rocked while I stared at the screen. I knew what came next—fuck, it was my story—but I wasn't sure I was ready to reveal it. But David's voice in my head was too loud to ignore.

"Get a grip. This is child's play."

Hearing voices wasn't anything new to me or my family. For that matter, neither was schizophrenia or schizoaffective disorder, which dropped a dose of depression into the equation. All it took was one past event to taint my family on the downside of the disease. And I guess in some respect, I understood. I wasn't a fan of Trevor, a command hallucination that fucked with all of us. Ticktock, my ass. Trevor was gone. His days of ticking and tocking anyone's clock were through. We all made sure of that.

That was why no one knew about David. No one knew because David was different. I was sure that was what every schizo claimed, but David *was* different. He wasn't like Trevor, and he never would be.

But to be clear, David wasn't some alternate personality like in the movie *Split*. It pissed me off when people got schizophrenia or schizoaffective mixed up with dissociative identity disorder. Even when I first suspected I may be schizophrenic and then learned about schizoaffective, I was never stupid enough to think my disease was like having multiple personalities.

"Idiots."

Agreed.

And don't even get me *started* on the depression. I could handle all the other shit if I didn't get so bummed out. I could be watching anime and suddenly start to tear up.

"How fucked up is that?"

Very fucked up.

I glanced behind me.

"Where's the cat?"

Dunno.

Anyway, when I heard David, it was like having a conversation with myself. I wasn't taking on the role of some new identity or different character. Schizo was messed up on its own without adding multiple personalities into the mix.

But just like most things, people attached themselves to one word, like hallucination, and automatically associated schizophrenia with split personalities when the two couldn't be more different. Someone with DID had a complete alternative personality, but with schizophrenia, it could be a visual or auditory hallucination.

I didn't see shit, but I did hear David. It was like hearing myself, but instead of talking to myself out loud—because who did that—I talked to David. That was what I called the voice when I first started hearing it, because it just made sense to give him a name.

Again, David wasn't my other personality or some alternate identity; he was just a voice—a voice in my head that I couldn't ignore, and I didn't want to. Everyone has a voice in their head. Mine was just a little louder.

David had always helped me see things differently. And as usual, he was right. This journal and what it revealed *was* child's play. Harmless. Besides, no matter what David thought I should write, I knew it was nothing more than a journal that no one would ever read, so I let him finish his thoughts.

A year or two passed, I remember seeing a bird's nest outside of our house. The birds chirping sounded pleasant to anyone else, but to me it was painful and irritating. I grabbed a rake and proceeded to knock down the nest and watch as the baby birds frantically scurried in hopes of returning to the shelter of their mother. I watched for thirty minutes until the last of the babies stopped squirming. This action did not bring me joy, hate, sadness, or anything a normal person might feel while watching something die. Instead, I felt excitement. To me, the witnessing of something dying was a rush and brought me adrenaline in a world that seemed so boring.

This was the first time I killed and, sadly, would not be the last.

CHAPTER 2

BRANSON

"TWENTY-TWO to base." The black handheld walkie-talkie looked like something my twin brother, Aaron, and I had when we were little and played spy games.

"This is base, go ahead," my boss, Jackson, responded.

"I've got a possible code ten." I tucked my baseball cap over my ears, but it didn't stop the wind from piercing my earlobes, which were numb. I stomped my feet on the snow-covered asphalt to keep them from freezing, but it only kicked up the white stuff. I knocked the snow off my boots against the tire of the silver Honda Accord and glanced at the information on my portable parking device. It contained the past history of university parking citations. The permit on the Accord's windshield was expired, and better yet, when I pulled up the car's history, there were eight unpaid citations.

Give 'em the boot.

"Can you state the license plate number?" Jackson always followed protocol.

"It's a Wyoming Bucking Bronco plate 2-1867," I said into the mic. My teeth practically chattered. *It's too fucking cold out here.*

"Please hold."

I took a step away in case the owner exited the football game early and headed toward his car. No reason for unnecessary confrontation. When it snowed last night, I thought for sure the game would be canceled, but leave it to Wyoming State University to clear the field for game day. Nothing mattered more to the university than keeping their top rank in the Mountain West Conference.

Jackson's voice broke through the frigid air. "Base to twenty-two, that's an affirmative code ten. What's your location?"

My heart raced. This was as exciting as it got for a college parking officer. "Stadium parking lot, north side."

I couldn't help but be pumped. *Hell yeah. This guy's got it coming. Add another sixty bucks to his unpaid citation and another point for me in the office parking pool.* The more tickets I wrote, the closer I got to the monthly bonus, which meant an extra hundred bucks in my wallet. I didn't know who the poor bastard was who would get the boot, but it didn't take a lot of common sense to pay your tickets or park legally.

I had at least ten minutes until Jackson arrived from the parking office with the boot that I'd attach to the rim of the tire. *No driving with that chunk of metal.*

The north side of the stadium was full of cars decorated with Wyoming State University bumper stickers. Snow didn't even stick to the glossy decals. "Wyoming Strong" in red lettering against a solid black background looked like blood from a fresh cut. The more I stared at the rows upon rows of glowing red letters, the more my adrenaline spiked. I may only be a part-time parking officer, but the authority I had gave me the power to ruin someone's day. And if I had to work in the butt cold, then I wasn't going to be alone in my misery.

A butter-yellow convertible bug with a light sprinkling of snow on its top looked prime for the picking. I checked the lower right side of their windshield and noticed they weren't displaying a permit. I pulled out my portable parking system and typed in their plate information.

Ugh, personal plates. They were always lame and stupid. I sounded out the vanity plates. "Q-T-E. Cutie?" The person driving this car was probably the opposite of their plates. The parking system showed they had no history, which meant only a warning. *Shit.*

I hit Print, and the portable printer slung across my shoulder spit out a parking warning that I tucked under the windshield wiper.

The Wyoming State vehicle that Jackson drove could be heard a block away. It was old and in need of repair, just like the campus. The only improvements the college ever made was to the athletics department. I could've run track, but I didn't want the added stress of training and trying to graduate.

These four years seemed to fly by. I still couldn't believe I was a college senior and was actually on course to graduate on time. Maybe I was like Aaron claimed, the eighth wonder of the world.

Aaron always gave me a hard time, but he was there for me when I needed him the most, so I ignored his constant put-downs and nicknames. My twin thought it was hilarious to call me "Jeffrey" after that psycho Jeffrey Dahmer. Even now it made me chuckle.

Jeffrey. What a douche.

Jackson hopped out of the black and red truck, which he towered over. He was six three, but his unstyled hair gave him an extra inch, and the red university jacket stretched across his biceps made him look even more massive than he was.

Jackson awkwardly grabbed the large boot from the back of the truck, which magnified his already awkward appearance. He hefted it toward the silver Accord and handed me two boot stickers that were neon orange. I cleared remnants of snow off the windshield and slapped one sticker on the glass and the other one on the driver window, then helped Jackson wrap the boot around the rim of the tire until it locked into place.

The sudden snap of the lock that secured the wheel clamp onto the car, permanently disabling it, reminded me of my friend Trevor and the hold he had on me. My shrink referred to Trevor as part of my psychosis, but he was no psychosis. Trevor was a darker version of me. When his voice became louder than my own, there was no freedom or control in my life. I was totally powerless. At one time, having Trevor call the shots was thrilling, but after he tried to break up my family, I decided our friendship had to end. But it wasn't easy. It took two turns in the psych ward before Trevor was out of my life.

The boot on the car was locked solidly in place. The only way the driver could get rid of the wheel clamp was for the owner to pay their dues.

It was the same with me and Trevor.

CHAPTER 3

AARON

"HEY, Jeffrey." I didn't have to wait long to hear my twin brother laugh over the phone.

"Fucker."

Even though we were attending two different colleges in two different states hundreds of miles apart, I knew he had a shit-eating grin on his face.

"Whatcha doing?" I asked as I walked across campus to my next class.

"Just chillin'."

I crested the snow-covered berm between the lower and upper campus, and the main international studies office came into view. Since I claimed international affairs as my degree, the majority of my classes were housed in a small wing of the psychology building, which seemed as random as the addition. The building looked like the bricks had been set in the sun before they were paved into place, their faded color making the three-story structure look older than it was. The additional tower attached to it looked like an afterthought, though the overall structure seemed rushed compared to the rest of the campus, which was built in the 1930s and felt collegiate.

Jefferson Heights University was a private college in Cleveland that catered to what my mom called "old money." The campus was filled with bronze statues of famous dead white guys and chapel-like structures that loomed over the grounds as if God himself was going to strike me down for my college sins. One-night stands truly had it rough when they walked back to their dorms.

"Don't you have class?" I said to my twin, who I would forever be parenting. Ever since we were young, I felt like I had to be the man of the house because I was the oldest, if only by a minute. Therefore, I was responsible for Branson.

"Nah, no classes today. I worked, and it was fucking freezing outside."

"Oh, that's right, you're the dick who ruins people's days," I said.

"Sad ticket issuer—that's me," Branson said with another laugh.

My cell chimed, and I glanced at the screen. "N-n-n-n-news." It was my daily update. I quickly checked the headlines. "Hey, did you hear that famous golf pro that Dad liked so much recently died."

"Yeah."

"He died of pneumonia," I said.

"So he suffered."

"Shut up, dude. That's fucked up." Branson's chuckle

sounded more like a wheeze.

"I bet all those fires in California started with one cigarette not being put out," I continued.

"Where are you getting this shit?" Branson said.

"I get all my news from Snapchat." I reached the building and saw a girl with long brown hair and a body with curves in all the right spots. She was a few steps ahead of me. I took the stairs two at a time to grab the door before she could and hold it open. When she smiled in my direction, I grinned. *Wow. Beautiful.*

"I hate Fox News. They suck," Branson said in my ear. "I'm not saying CNN is any better, but they are."

That time I laughed, and she slightly turned. I raised an eyebrow, and her face flushed. I walked behind her as she headed toward the main tower. She nervously glanced over her shoulder.

"I swear I'm not following you," I said, pulling the phone away from my ear.

She giggled, and her hair bounced on her shoulders. *Total dime.*

"Snapchat has all the news," I said while I watched her ass sway in a pair of black yoga pants that stretched tight across her heart-shaped ass.

"But Snapchat, really?" Branson actually seemed interested in something other than Pokémon Go.

"Yeah, bro. When they report on the Middle East, they don't refer to everyone as Muslims. They refer to them as Arabs."

"Oh, that's right. 'I'm Aaron Kovac. I went to Jordan

and studied abroad for a semester.'"

Again, I didn't have to be there to visualize my brother rolling his eyes. His tone said it all.

"Hey, bro, don't forget that October is breast cancer awareness month," he said.

That made me laugh. "Little brother, it's kind of hard to miss with all the pink crap all over campus."

"None of the sororities do anything for breast cancer on our campus. But my buddy told me they hold events at Albany County Community College."

"And?" My twin took forever to get to the point.

"And I think it'd be really cool if we supported the sorority or whatever group on campus and pitch in some money for breast cancer awareness," he said.

"Yeah, that's not my thing."

"Now who's being a dick? Aaron, it might not be your thing, but it is Mom's."

Branson paused long enough to piss me off, as if I needed time to reflect. *What the fuck?*

"Hey, when's the last time you called Mom?" he asked.

No matter how many times we spoke—which was almost daily—my brother always asked about our mom, as if her cancer diagnosis was news to me. The more I saw pink ribbons around campus, the more I wanted to rip every single one down. The groups and sororities didn't care if it was breast cancer or foot fungus; they had their do-good quota to fill so they could go back to being assholes and idiots. *No thanks.*

I sighed. "Listen, Bran, I call her about every week.

I think I spoke to her yesterday. Don't worry, I'm still checking in on her."

"Dude, it's not about checking in on her." Branson's tone was as agitated as I felt. "It's about making sure she knows you care."

"I do care!" I snapped. "I gotta go, bro."

"Hey."

His voice stopped me from ending the call.

"What?" I exhaled.

"Do you like me, Bert?"

Despite my anger, I smiled. When we were little, our go-to show was *Sesame Street* and our favorite characters were Bert and Ernie. I was Bert, the boring, serious, smart one with the unibrow, and Branson was Ernie, the shorter, funnier, oblivious one with the harebrained ideas that always backfired on poor Bert. We watched certain episodes over and over, but our favorite one was about friendship. We memorized the lines before we even knew our alphabet.

"So... do you like me, Bert?" he said again, and I knew I'd never get off the phone until I played along.

"You know people think they're gay, right?" I said.

"Doesn't matter," he said and then jumped right back into character. "Do you like me, Bert?"

I shook my head. "Do I like you? Of course I like you, Ernie. You're my best friend."

"You're mine too."

No one could piss me off more quickly or make me happier faster than Branson. He really was my best friend.

"Okay, little brother, I've gotta go."

I ended the call and walked to my class, where I took my regular seat in the back of the room. My mind jumped back to our conversation and bounced from thought to thought.

They think I don't care? I'm trying. This distance shit is hard. They never check on me and tell me they care. I just know they do. I don't need confirmation. And I don't need to go to some cancer fundraiser to remind me that my mom's dying.

Professor Whitman assumed her post in the lecture hall. From my seat in the last row, I stared at her. She always wore black, which matched her wiry hair and made her skinny, pale frame seem even thinner. Her large Harry Potter-like glasses didn't help her look at all. If it wasn't for her bright personality, she could get mistaken for a witch.

When her PowerPoint presentation on the Israeli-Palestinian conflict began, my focus shifted off her and to the slides. Better still, thoughts of my conversation with Branson disappeared.

CHAPTER 4

DAVID AND ME

"**BONITA,** where are you?" My voice was as forceful as the way I slammed the door to my apartment. I scanned the living room for my cat, but she was nowhere to be found.

"Probably better. You have too much to do."

Agreed.

I tossed my baseball cap on the couch, combed through my hair with my fingers, grabbed a beer from the mini fridge, and took a seat in front of my laptop. My journal was waiting for me. And so was David. His voice seemed louder and more urgent.

A Killer's Journal

When I was growing up through elementary and middle school, I never really had a lot of friends.

I remember watching other kids around my age and being curious about how to be like them and how to become friends with people like them. For the life of me, I couldn't figure out how to be normal and how to make friends. I always had my twin brother, but outside of that, I had no one.

However, even though I felt that way, I was never sad or upset because I had David. I couldn't really understand what David was saying or even what he looked like, but he was always there. As soon as I woke up until the time I went to bed, he always lingered in my head. David and I understood each other.

"It's funny how your mom always says that twins have each other. Do they?"

I shrugged and took a swig of beer. *Good question.* I continued typing.

Don't get me wrong. I love my twin brother, but he wasn't always there. He *was too interested in fitting in and being popular. Not like David. David wanted the same fulfillment that I found in killing small animals like the baby birds. Those sorts of actions made sense to me, and I often found myself fantasizing about the deaths of fellow students who made me mad or picked on me.*

As often as I thought about how I would cause those deaths, I just as equally thought about the repercussions. When I thought about the aftermath, I knew I could never abandon my family, especially not my twin brother, so those fantasies remained just that—fantasies.

My throat felt tight. I drained the beer and reached behind me to the mini fridge to grab another. The more I drank, the stronger David's voice became, so I cracked the beer and took a hearty gulp before I continued my entry.

What I discovered was that over time, my imagination became much more mature. Instead of thinking about senseless killings, I began to orchestrate plans and strategies to kill without getting caught. Those thoughts kept my brain occupied enough where I didn't have to lash out and hurt others or things. The feelings for those types of actions still excited me, but I could never carry out my plans.

But David... he was another story. David began to become more vivid, and instead of just a cloud of darkness, I began hearing his voice. It came like a buzzing in my head, and while I still couldn't really understand what he was saying, it became clear what his role was in my life.

CHAPTER 5

AARON

"HEY, Ma, I'm making your mac and cheese recipe—you know, add more butter, no milk," I said when I answered her call.

"Uh-huh," she said as if I hadn't spoken.

Uh-huh? It was a placeholder for what she really wanted to talk about.

"So what's up?" I asked.

"Well, my oncologist said it'd be okay if I worked part-time. Of course, as soon as he said that, he placed me on a new medication, so we'll see. But for now, the legislative services office needed some help, and they chose me."

"Ma, that's great. So you're working with LSO?"

Her voice seemed to perk up. "I am. It's amazing I even got hired with the way I look, and… well, there's my reputation…." The sudden lift in her tone shifted, and it felt like someone elbowed me in the stomach.

"Ma, that happened four years ago. *And* you were smart enough to move away. What happened at that shithole college in Casper isn't news in the state's capital. The city of Cheyenne is progressive. They don't care if you tanked *one* early admission applicant. Ashley Bailey got into Wyoming State University *and* got to carry on the Bailey tradition. Shit, she's about to graduate with Branson, so what you did is old news—if it ever was news to begin with."

"Aaron, I appreciate your optimism, but when I purposefully targeted Senator Bailey's daughter, it *was* a thing in the state's capital. The man's charming, arrogant, and has enough handlers around him to remind him that I'm the one who almost torpedoed his daughter's chance of carrying on the family tradition."

"So he's basically a career politician. Shit, Ma, there's nothing new about that."

Her laughter was good to hear. My mom hadn't laughed much since her regular mammogram appointment turned into a three-year battle against breast cancer.

I swallowed, but the knot in my throat wouldn't go away. *Focus. She needs you to be strong.*

"Ma, Senator Bailey's only popular because he's an anomaly. He's a second-term Democratic senator in a red state," I said.

"Aaron, where would I be without you?"

I would do anything for you.

When I didn't say anything, my mom did what she always did and filled in the silence.

"Well, sweetie, I called because I was hoping you could

explain how the legislature passes a bill and stuff like that, because that looks like what I'll be helping with."

I smiled. *I know this.* While I explained to my mom how the Wyoming House of Representatives and Senate worked, the pot of water reached the boiling point, and I dumped the box of macaroni into it. I liked helping her. I'd bet money she was taking notes while I gave her a broad overview of how the legislative process worked.

My knowledge of Wyoming legislative procedures was based off a summer at Wyoming Boys' State, an annual event for high schoolers across the state. For one week in June, I got to serve as state auditor and learn firsthand how the government worked and how to enact laws. Boys' State was known for its emphasis on civic engagement and turning out future leaders.

Of course, my idiot twin brother referred to my weeklong summer event as nothing more than a group of political history nerds in a circle jerk. Still, I learned a lot about politics.

"Sweetheart, all of this is so helpful," she said when I stopped talking. "And really, *you* should have this job instead of me."

I laughed.

"I'm serious. Have you ever thought of returning to Wyoming?"

"Hold on, Ma, I've got to lower the heat on the stove. I don't want the water spilling over the side." I turned the dial.

"Good for you," she said. "There's nothing worse than

over- or under-cooking mac and cheese. Either way, you end up with soggy or crunchy noodles. And who likes a soggy noodle?"

I laughed as my mom chuckled at her own bad joke.

"Sweetie, I'm sorry to bug you on the start of your weekend," she said. "This whole legislation stuff is Greek to me." She exhaled, and her frustration grew louder. "And my new boss expects me to know how the legislature operates and what to expect, and I don't have a clue." Her voice dropped, and I could tell the newness of it all—the job, the legislature, her boss—bothered her.

"Ma, don't stress. You always end up on your feet."

She half laughed, and I knew it was for my sake.

"If you don't like working at LSO, you should quit."

That time her laughter sounded like her. My ma had this crazy laugh that was goofy as hell, but it always made me think of happier times, a time before schizophrenia and cancer imploded the life I knew and the people I loved most.

"Uh, that's not quite how it works, son. When you have a mortgage payment, tuition times two, and two other children at home who like to eat, you go to work, even if it's part-time."

My mom tanked her career at the college because of Trevor, my twin brother's crazy delusion, who took over his thinking during his senior year of high school. It took a full year *after* we discovered who and what Trevor was before Branson eventually got Trevor under control, but not until after he'd fucked up his senior year and my mom's livelihood.

Fucking Trevor.

My cell phone beeped, alerting me that there was a call waiting. "Hey, Ma, hold on." I glanced at the screen. "Branson's on the other line."

"Oh, tell him I said hi," she told me before I switched over.

"Hey, bro, what's up?" I drained the macaroni in the colander that was perched in the sink and tore the cheese packet open with my mouth.

"I'm just hanging out at the apartment," he said. "Whatcha doing?"

"I've got Mom on the other line. You okay?" I poured the drained pasta back into the pot and added a spoonful of butter before I sprinkled the cheesy packet of goodness into the mix. People ruined mac and cheese by adding milk. All you needed for perfect mac and cheese was a spoonful of butter and the cheese packet. A cheap, fatty college meal made in an instant. Tasty vittles ahead. "You got any plans for this weekend?"

"Nothing much, just homework and working," Branson said.

"Yeah, sometimes I wish I was still there," I said of Wyoming State University, which I attended for two years.

"Well, you're the idiot who decided to switch schools for a girl," Branson said jokingly.

But it wasn't funny. It pissed me off that everyone in my family, including my twin, was under the assumption that I transferred colleges for some girl. She wasn't even part of the equation. The reality was that I moved away so I wouldn't have to be my brother's keeper anymore.

Yet here I am.

"Hey, Jeffrey, can I call you later?" I asked.

He chuckled, and I grinned.

"Yeah, sounds good. Talk to you then."

When I switched back to my mom, I knew the first words out of her mouth would be about Branson.

"So, how's Bran doing?" she asked when I knew what she *really* wanted to know was whether my identical half was sane or not.

"He's doing great, Ma." I paused, knowing she'd still worry. "And so am I," I added, not that it would mean anything. Ever since Trevor entered our lives, my mom was consumed with Branson's well-being. She had four kids but only one she focused all her attention on. I was a resource and reassurance, not someone she worried or seemed concerned about.

"That's wonderful," she said, clearly not hearing me.

That empty, left-out feeling sank to the pit of my stomach. My role in this fucked-up family was to be the caregiver to my twin. And when I wasn't taking care of his sorry ass, I had my mom to consider. I loved Branson, but we were twenty-one years old and in our senior years of college. When was my mom going to realize that Branson was an adult in charge of his mental health and his life? When was she going to get it that if he stayed on his meds and saw his doctor, he'd be fine? When was she going to stop babying him?

Hell, for that matter, when is she going to see me?

I glanced at the pot of cheesy noodles. Suddenly the thought of mac and cheese turned my stomach.

"Hey, Ma, if you don't have any more questions regarding the legislature, I'm going to go." I dumped my dinner into the trash can.

"Oh." The drop in her voice actually sounded like she cared.

"Ma, you're going to do great. LSO is lucky to have you."

"Aaron, seriously, where would I be without you?" she said, and I knew she meant it. My family relied on me, and normally I was okay with it. Lately it was just getting to me. But that wasn't part of the script. My role was to act like everything was okay.

"Ma, anytime I can help...." I didn't have to finish the sentence because it was assumed. I was the helper, the go-to guy, the fixer. "Hey, listen, sorry to cut this short, but I have a lot of homework."

"Senior year, kid. You're almost through. And just think, a double major." My mom couldn't mask her love of education, and in that respect, I always got her attention. Didn't matter that having a double major about killed me; I was at the top of my class, and no one—not even Branson or the evil third twin, Trevor—could ruin that.

"I'm so proud of you," she said, and I couldn't help but smile. It didn't matter how old I got, getting her approval meant more to me than anyone else's.

"Thanks, Ma. Love you."

"Love you more, son. Thanks for all your help this evening."

"Anytime."

I hung up the phone, grabbed my backpack, and headed out. It was Friday night, and there was no reason to stay home. Besides, I needed to clear my head.

CHAPTER 6

BRANSON

I hated living in Casper. There was nothing here for me. Ever since Aaron left our sophomore year, college just wasn't the same. And it wasn't like I was dating anyone. After Dakota and I broke up, it felt like I couldn't find my groove again. And we broke up years ago. *Lame.*

"Hey, Bran, want to go to a Broncos game? We're going to stay in Denver tonight and catch the game tomorrow. Gen admission is cheap."

The guy across the hall from my apartment was always inviting me out even though I rarely, if ever, accepted.

"Nah, I'm good. I've got homework." The disadvantage to our apartment complex was that in the winter, the air conditioning blew, and in the summer, the heater did. We all lived with our doors open to try and regulate the temperature to something normal. Tonight it was erring on the cold side, so of course the air conditioner seemed to be in full swing.

"Maybe next time," my neighbor said.

I nodded toward the hallway between us. "Yeah."

I didn't want to go to Denver or the game, but I also didn't want to hang around my apartment alone. Anywhere was better than here.

I grabbed my keys and backpack and decided to find something more stimulating to do on a Friday night.

And I knew just the cure.

CHAPTER 7

DAVID AND ME

I'D always heard that even if identical twins were separated at birth, the odds of finding the other were good because of the similarities. I didn't know if that was true. But it was Friday night, and I wasn't sure what my twin was doing. I only knew that when David suggested coffee, I knew what I'd be doing.

The coffeehouse on campus was located in a really small red brick building, but what Java Joes lacked inside, it made up for outside. The patio space was large with circular tables that had umbrellas, except in the fall and winter when the umbrellas were replaced with heat lamps. You wouldn't think a heat lamp could ward off the freezing temperatures, but damn if they didn't shelter us from the cold. And tonight was no exception.

It was only October, but when the frost in the morning didn't thaw until late afternoon, it was an all-day kind of cold. It was the kind of cold that stuck to you.

I took my mug of black coffee to a back corner table and sat with my backpack beside me. Pulling out my laptop, I opened it so my screen faced away from glaring eyes. No one could see what I was working on, but I could see everyone.

A girl with a high-pitched voice was discussing some bullshit gossip to someone on the phone. A blonde in tight yoga pants made me wish I was sitting beside her and not the douche she was with. Still, she glanced in my direction, and I casually returned my focus to my laptop. A fraternity jock, who was clearly the top in the social circles, looked like he didn't give two shits about the cute brunette he was with, and it pissed me off.

I pulled up the journal entry and began taking notes. Or rather David did. His voice propelled my thoughts; I was simply his stenographer. He spoke and I typed.

Factor: Girl on the phone

Weaknesses: Alone, doesn't look like she'd put up a fight, easy to take down. Plus, she doesn't look smart enough to carry pepper spray.

Threats: Other people. She doesn't look like she'd go into an alley by herself.

Anyone reading over my shoulder would think I wanted

to rape the girl, but that couldn't be further from the truth. I got pleasure from the *idea* of burying a knife in someone's throat, nothing more.

Factor: Hot girl in yoga pants.

Weaknesses: She looks like a sorority girl, so she's probably drunk all the time and would be easy to pick off.

Threats: Boyfriend. She's probably always with him.

I took a sip of coffee.

"This is a great coffee shop. And cheap too. You wouldn't think that. It's probably one of the few places on campus that's not overpriced."

Agreed. I took another look around the place and resumed typing.

Factor: The fraternity jock

Weaknesses: He thinks so highly of himself that he wouldn't think he'd leave himself vulnerable. Plus, he's well built, so he probably thinks he's untouchable.

Strengths: Well built.

Of the three choices, the girl on the phone was my best bet. Theoretically.

"It wouldn't be that hard. One puncture to the throat with a knife or the tip of a pen and walk away casually like nothing happened."

My adrenaline spiked, and the fall evening air no longer had a bite to it. Scoping, planning, and theorizing about actually taking down a person on my list made life bearable. David looked for things that upset me and needed fixing. That girl with the high-pitched voice on the phone fit the bill.

I watched her, waiting for her to finish her annoying phone call. I'd wait all night if I had to.

"You into that girl?"

I flinched and glanced over my laptop screen to the petite, brown-haired, wide-eyed woman I'd met last weekend at a bar.

"It's about time you showed up. I thought you were ditching me," I said with a devil-may-care smile that I knew worked well with women. Seeing her snapped me back to reality. And just like that, David's voice disappeared and all I heard was her voice, which was softer than I remembered.

When I stood to give her a hug, I closed my laptop and any further surveillance for the night ended.

"Sorry I was so late. I was caught up in a work meeting," she said when our brief hug ended.

"No worries. I was just working on a paper."

She pulled out the chair beside mine, and the smell of vanilla, like warm cookies fresh out of the oven, filtered between us. She was cute, sweet, and she seemed interested in me.

"How are your classes going?" I took a sip of my coffee. "You're in your last year, right?"

"That's right," she said, "and I'm ready to be done."

"Me too. Just a semester and a half left, and then we're free to grow up and pay off our student loans."

Her laughter was unexpected. Instead of a high-pitched, annoying squeak, she had more of a giggle that was refreshingly pleasant.

"Hey, you want to get out of here and study at my place?" I asked.

"A first date and you're already taking me home?" she said with a wink.

"Don't worry, I intend to study, but if you think of anything else to do, just let me know," I said in a flirtatious way.

I left ten bucks under my coffee cup for the unlucky soul charged with our cleanup. Plus, I always liked to tip well in front of a girl. There were a lot of things I was guilty of, but being a shitty tipper wasn't one of them. As we left the patio, I held the door for my study date and the annoying girl on the phone, who decided to leave at the same time. She glanced at me, and when she thanked me, her voice no longer sounded irritating.

A full moon cast its light, making our walk to my apartment well lit.

"Oh, I didn't know this was where you lived," she said as we approached my apartment building. "Isn't there a shortcut through the alley?"

I shrugged. "Yeah, but you never know who or what may be lurking in an alleyway."

She elbowed me. "Like you have to worry about that."

"But I do." The fear in my voice betrayed me, and she glanced up at me with something I rarely saw—compassion.

"Don't worry, big guy, I'm here." She gave me a wink that warmed me from the inside out.

"Hey, I wasn't joking about the studying," I said as we stood in front of my building. "I actually have a ten-page paper that's due Monday."

For a moment I wondered if she'd bail. Instead, her adorable giggle followed me up the stairs to my apartment.

CHAPTER 8

BRANSON

THE beauty of a one-night stand was waking up alone. Optimally, they worked best if two components were met: an older woman with her own place. There was the occasional crashing at my place like last night, but I always made sure they left afterward. An older woman didn't mind, but hooking up with someone my age always resulted in the residue of hurt feelings and more damage to my reputation. But thirty-year-old women were different. No thirty-year-old wanted a commitment from a twenty-one-year-old. Nor did they want to stay the night. They knew what was up and didn't ask for anything more than they knew they were getting—a night of no-strings-attached fucking.

I locked the door to my apartment, tucked my phone into my jacket pocket, and headed toward my car.

No worries about her calling. I learned early on that, besides finding a woman in her thirties, the more important rule was not exchanging any personal info like my number.

That way they couldn't stalk me later.

Not that I'd really mind if this one did. Her body was rockin'. No kids. No commitments. She was in the prime of knowing what she wanted. And it didn't hurt that when I first met her at the bar, she'd picked up the tab. I wasn't going to let her, but she insisted, and when she pulled out her platinum card, who was I to stop her?

I didn't even mind that she was on campus to finish her degree. She wasn't some clingy, needy woman. And the thought of future study sessions wasn't bad.

The sun banked off the snow berm and nearly blinded me. *Fuck, that's bright.*

What wasn't as bright was my faded green Saab that looked about as clean as the dirty slush around my tires. I got into my old ice bucket and realized the car parked behind me was up my ass.

I hate Casper. People suck.

I heard Aaron in my head. He'd tell me not to hang with shady people. What he didn't realize was that they were all shady. They all sucked. The sooner I was through with college, the better. I backed up, and by sheer luck, I didn't hit the fucktard's car.

I headed toward I-25 and Cheyenne. There wasn't anything for me in Casper. Weekends were the worst. Before I reached Glenrock and its dead zone, I texted my sister, Carson.

On way to c u guys n mom. Don't tell her. Wna surprise her.

Carson relied on selfies to answer. A pic of my teenaged

sister with her chin pointed toward her chest in an attempt to have a double chin made me laugh. She was way too skinny to pull it off.

She was another reason I tried to get home when school and work allowed. I liked treating her and Jack to things that made me feel good when I was bummed out. And nothing made someone forget their troubles—if even for a moment—than a Loaf 'N Jug run. Soda, chips, and candy, lots and lots of candy. Or, as my little brother, Jack, always said, "The start to diabetes."

It also didn't hurt that I liked our new home in Cheyenne. Well, it wasn't new, but it was to us. My mom was so proud when she found a house that didn't require a thousand repairs. It was smaller and older than our home in Casper, but it felt homier. Thanks to me, my mom lost her high-paying job. I knew she didn't blame me, but I did.

If only I had gotten Trevor under control.

If only I had realized how much control he had over my thoughts and actions.

If only. If the road to hell was paved with good intentions, then purgatory was tiled with if-onlys.

The drive from Casper to Cheyenne was normally two and a half hours that I made in two. The less time in my head, the better. Besides, the sooner I got home, the quicker I got to my mom. She had her second clean mammogram screen recently, and it was time to celebrate the last two and a half years of hell.

At first when she got cancer, nothing big happened. It wasn't like she suddenly lost her hair or looked sick.

Even after her first surgery, she still appeared and acted like my mom. Then a month passed before I got to head home again, and when I saw her after her second surgery, her energy had shifted. By her third surgery, the mom I knew had all but vanished. It was like she'd given up. She was either in bed or the bathroom, sleeping or throwing up. Jack was constantly beside her patting her bald head. I bought her one of those pink scarves, hoping she'd wear it, but she said it made her hot. Her head was the color of puke, like her whole body swallowed up her sickness. What I didn't understand was why she wasn't bouncing back to normal. She still looked sick, which made no sense.

I shuddered. When my mom was diagnosed with cancer, it was the worst time in my life—even worse than Trevor. Aaron moved away, which was what I bet my sister and little brother wanted. But Carson and Jack were home. They were on the frontlines and saw her decline daily.

I wanted to be home, but my mom insisted I stay in school and finish what I'd started and Trevor tried to prevent. She wanted to know I was living free from Trevor when she wasn't even living at all. There was a time not too long ago when I was sure her life was slipping away, which just about broke me.

Tears stung my eyes at the memories. There wasn't a day that I didn't think about my mom and wish it had happened to me.

I rolled down the window and the cold air bit my face. It hurt, but anything was better than reliving those feelings. I couldn't lose her. Not now. Not when I finally had my shit together.

I turned on the radio, and one of my mom's favorite songs was playing. I shook my head. My shrink would remind me that there was no running away from feelings, but listening to Darius Rucker sing a country song crossed the line. I changed the channel, and the funky hard sound of Twenty-One Pilots and their existential, vein-spilling lyrics about turning back time to the good old days made me laugh.

"Okay, you win," I said to this higher power thing I'd discovered during my second stint in the crazy hospital.

I went from severe depression, hallucinations, and feeling like I'd never have a future to having the pain slowly subside with treatment. Under the hospital's lock and key, I learned coping skills to function with my symptoms and live with schizoaffective disorder.

It was like that with my mom's cancer. Just as soon as it entered our lives, it seemed to leave. Or she decided to fight it. I honestly didn't know. All I knew was that her medical team said she was in remission, and if cancer taught me anything, it was to take the small victories when they came.

She didn't know it yet, but I regularly donated plasma for money. In the last two months, I had a Visa card loaded with enough to take us all out to dinner to celebrate.

But there was one stop I had to make first.

The table wasn't in the center of campus like I expected. Instead, the signs for the event led to the college pub. I'd barely set foot into the bar when a host of sorority girls cheered.

"Welcome!" they said in unison, and I felt like I had won the lottery.

I tried to hide my smile and embarrassment, but it was impossible. I wasn't the kind of guy who had women cheer when I walked into a room.

I headed toward the only table draped in pink. Mason jars painted in varying shades with matching pink carnations were scattered across the table. A pink cowboy boot with a white ribbon that read "Give Cancer The Boot" was positioned in the center of the table.

A row of pink T-shirts and stress-reliever balls immediately caught my eye.

"Hey," I said when I approached.

Four of the five women smiled brightly and returned my greeting. The fifth woman, who sat with two sorority sisters on either side of her, didn't smile or speak. The only part of her name tag that was visible read "Chair" in bright pink letters.

I'd bet my plasma money she's the philanthropy chair—a thankless position in Greek life. And by the looks of it, no fraternity on campus wanted to partner with her. Shocking.

She pointed her nails that matched her name tag toward me. "Branson Kovak."

I took a step back.

"You don't remember me, do you?" The quasi leader of the all-blonde tribe kept her green eyes locked on mine with laser focus.

I slightly shrugged and gave her my best don't-kill-me look.

She burst out laughing, and I began to relax. Then she turned to her sisters. "This is Branson. He's schizophrenic." She shot me a look. "That's it, isn't it, Branson? Schizophrenia?"

It wasn't the first time someone from the past mentioned my mental illness in public, but it was the way she did it, like an accusation, that made it feel like all my blood drained from my body.

Who the fuck is she?

I slowly nodded, not sure what to say next.

"Yeah, he used to date one of my friends." She glared at me and tossed her shoulder-length blonde hair with a smugness that let me know she wasn't the queen bee for nothing. "Dakota? You totally fucked her over when you went all psycho on her."

Oh, right. I remember her now.

"That's fair," I said to her disbelief. "I made things right with Dakota, but you're right. When I was in my illness, I was a real jerk."

"*Jerk*? Try asshole. You called Dakota 'rez trash' at a party in front of *everyone*. It was the first and only time I met you, or whoever you were, and I'd hoped it'd be the last." She crossed her arms over her barely there boobs, her green eyes flashing with anger. "Dakota's family tie to the reservation was a low blow, but"—she shrugged—"what can you expect from a psycho."

"Actually, I have schizoaffective disorder. There's a

depressive component. I'm doubly blessed," I said as a way of hopefully diffusing the situation.

"Whatever. You're still whack," she said with a roll of her eyes.

I took a slow, steady breath. "I *used* to be. But I take a handful of meds daily, see a shrink monthly, and show up for life at Wyo State, which is why I'm *still* stuck in Casper." I slowly smiled. "Now *that's* whack."

Four of the five women laughed. "That's so great," one of them said. "My dad is bipolar. He did the same thing as you—you know, taking meds and stuff—and he's so much better."

Another of the sorority sisters chimed in then. "My brother was a cutter. Weird, right?" She shook her blonde hair. "But after he went to this inpatient treatment center, he's a *totally* different guy."

But the chair of the feel-good event remained unimpressed. "Whatever. If you go to Wyo State, why are you *here*?"

I had to play this right to get what I needed. Albany County Community College was what my mom referred to as a "junior college for average students," which was a total slam to my high school friends who didn't have the grades to get into Wyoming's only four-year university. I doubted I had the grades either, but my mom used whatever pull she'd still had four years ago to ensure I had a spot. Still, the rivalry was real.

"You'd think Wyo State would have the best of the best, right?" I said.

Four of the sisters nodded.

"Well, they don't, because with all the sororities on campus, there isn't one that celebrates breast cancer awareness month. Crazy, right?" I instantly regretted the use of crazy. *Fuck.*

"Are you for real?" she who had no name but Chair spoke again.

"Legit. Even the sorority we partner with," I said in Greek speak to let them all know I wasn't a goddamn independent. "Their philanthropic work is heart health." I held my hand against my chest. "Hey, I'm all about women's heart health, but I'm *pretty* sure breast cancer claims more women's lives." I gripped the table and leaned in for total effect. "That's why I'm here. My mom's been battling breast cancer...." Suddenly, I felt myself lose my hold on the table. I let go and took a quick step back.

For all my efforts to have maximum impact, my inability to maintain my composure along with my voice breaking had more of an effect than even I'd intended. I cleared my throat, but fuck if I didn't sound like I was about to cry. *Get it together, Bran.*

"Uh, anyway, I drove to Cheyenne from Casper because my mom lives here now. And it's where she has her cancer care. I wanted to walk into the house tonight wearing one of your shirts to show her my support."

Before I could reach into my back pocket for my wallet, the woman on the end of the table, the one whose brother was a cutter, pushed her chair out, walked over to me, and wrapped her arms around me.

"I'm so sorry," she said, and her tenderness almost gutted me.

"Whatever." The philanthropy chair scoffed, jarring me back to reality. Some people would always see me as damaged.

Then she threw a T-shirt toward me. "We don't carry extra-large, so hopefully this'll fit."

I clenched my teeth. It was one thing to call me psycho, but to attack my weight? That shit hit closer to home. *If I wasn't on all these meds, I wouldn't have to worry about my fucking weight, you stupid cow.* But I squelched the urge to verbally vomit all over her. Why give her more reason to hate me?

I slowly exhaled, reached into my wallet, and placed a hard-earned twenty into the boot. The boot was what I'd like to give her if she ever parked on a real college campus. Shaking my head at the thought to cover my slight smile, I refocused on the task at hand.

"Would it be possible to get a T-shirt for my mom?" I hated sounding so pathetic, but if it meant a shirt for my mom, I'd grovel and look like a complete loser if I had to.

I wanted to get a couple for Carson and Jack too, but asking for two more ran the risk of the chair completely losing her shit.

"Of course." The one who had hugged me grabbed a shirt and a handful of the pink stress-reliever balls and gently handed them to me.

"Thank you." There wasn't anything more to say. I took my armful of pink mementos and headed toward the door.

CHAPTER 9

BRANSON

WHEN my shrink, Dr. Cordova, relocated to Iowa, he referred me to Dr. Blaze. Blaze had offices in Casper and Cheyenne, though I usually met him in Cheyenne. The less time in Casper the better.

I signed the clipboard that sat in the tray in the glass partition and stole a glance at Hope. She was a ginger, but her hair wasn't flaming red. It was this blend of red and blonde. Still, I wondered if the saying were true: "red on the head, fire in bed." I choked down a chuckle. Her skin was pale with freckles across the bridge of her nose that I couldn't stop staring at. The little strip was like a constellation that pointed me directly to her striking blue eyes. She looked away from her computer screen and slid across the glass panel that separated us, and when she smiled, I thought my knees would give out.

"Branson. How ya doing?"

"Not bad. Going to see my mom after this."

"Oh, how is she?" She leaned forward, and so did her cleavage. Milky skin poured out of her lacy bra.

I cleared my throat. "Good. She's good." I stared at her like an idiot, not knowing what to say next.

"I'm glad to hear that. Say hi to her for me."

I nodded. My mom used to come to my appointments with me. It was our agreement when I went off my meds for a second time. I got it. I'd be worried too. But once she got cancer, the hour-long appointments were just too much on her.

The familiar pain settled in my throat once more. When my mom got cancer, it was like my throat stopped working. I couldn't swallow without it hurting, and whenever I spoke about it, my voice cracked or didn't work at all, just like what happened in the bar with those sorority girls. Hope was probably the only person I could talk to about my mom without that happening, though I barely knew her.

"Yeah, I'm taking her out to dinner tonight. She passed her last two mammogram scans."

Hope's face practically sparkled, and the grip around my throat lessened. "Branson, that's so great."

"Thanks." I was about to ask her if she wanted to join us when I heard Ester call my name. Ester was a nice but extremely hefty nurse. I'd tackled linesmen who were smaller, which was why I never messed with her. I nodded toward Hope with the invitation lingering on my lips, which was exactly where it stayed. I followed Ester as she waddled toward the doctor's office.

Dr. Blaze didn't look like his name suggested. There was

no glow, flash, or fire to his clothes or voice. Nor was he a ginger like Hope. He had this super-mellow hippie vibe going on.

"Everything's good, man" was his go-to line.

It didn't matter if I told him that the shadow people were crafting a battalion of crazies in my head ready to take over the world. As far as Dr. Blaze was concerned, everything was good.

His office was an extension of the man. His décor and furniture had to date back to the seventies. I didn't even think Goodwill would accept his shit as a donation. There was also this gurgling waterfall thing on a side table that was irritating as fuck. But the Sunday school–type quote that hung on the wall was the real kicker. I was sure it was meant to be inspirational, but it wasn't.

The journey is more important than the destination.

The frame looked like it'd been through a rough journey. The wooden edges were nicked, and the glass was dull and yellowed. A desk with some diplomas on the wall was pushed toward the back of the room like an afterthought. The brown, fake suede couch was like every other therapy couch I'd sat on—saggy in the middle, but not in a comfortable, reassuring way. More like an "I'm stuck and how the hell am I going to get my big ass out of this" thing.

Dr. Blaze parked his skinny hippie ass in the matching brown side chair beside his desk. In brown cords and a tan shirt, he blended in with the room and the large stain on the ceiling above him. It seemed to grow every month. It always made me wonder if the roof was going to fall in on us both. Or perhaps it already had.

Dr. Blaze was smart. For all his laid-back approach, the guy didn't miss a beat.

"Your blood work looks good," he said, skimming through my file, the size of which rivaled one of my mom's textbooks.

Monthly blood draws ensured that I was, indeed, taking my antipsychotic medication. After I'd kept the return of Trevor and my auditory hallucinations of him hidden from everyone following my first hospitalization, they'd started monitoring my blood monthly.

It wasn't like I couldn't rig the test if I wanted to. I knew guys on campus who worked part-time in the lab and were as cash poor as me, selling their plasma to afford the shitload of medical textbooks they had to buy while studying to be phlebotomists. It wouldn't take much money to convince them to alter the lab results.

It basically boiled down to trust in the end. Was I actually being honest? So I did the monthly draws to allay my mom's fears and rebuild her trust. I got it. Schizophrenia influenced how I thought, felt, and behaved. Add in the depressive component and my mind was like a loaded weapon.

"You look good." Blaze closed the folder with my name labeled on the side.

"Yeah, I lost the last ten pounds I gained four years ago." I laughed.

"Well, you're staying active and you look good. How's your social life?"

"I think it's going to be like the last ten pounds. It's going to take a while," I said, which made my shrink chuckle.

I liked Blaze. He reminded me of my high school counselor, Clive. Both were easy to talk to, and they really seemed to care about me. I wasn't just another name on their schedule. Plus, both Clive and Blaze seemed to understand what I was going through and realized that not all schizophrenics were the same.

Blaze reached behind him and placed my folder on the stack already on his desk. One good sneeze and that shit was coming down. I wasn't the most organized person, but compared to Blaze, I had OCD.

"You know, Branson, I've seen a lot worse cases than what you've had. Plus, you're doing all the right things." He paused, and I glanced at the crack in the wall. *Why doesn't he patch that shit?*

"You're still active in the fraternity's executive council, right?"

"Yeah, I just got reelected."

"Which position are you now?"

"Secretary." It was one of the few things that didn't suck about college.

"That's positive. Sometimes with the diagnosis of schizoaffective, people are kind of more socially isolated. Or rather social isolation occurs, but you don't really fit that piece. You're interactive. You're busy with school and the fraternity and work. Those are all very positive. You're still working for the parking patrol?"

"Yup, I'm still the sad-ticket issuer."

Again, he obliged my lame humor with a chuckle.

"Still, those are all real positive things. And then if we were to look at your mental health history, where you've had these episodes, and if we really went back and looked at every time you had an episode, I would assume they were all more related to some sort of stress response."

"Yeah, it's usually stress related," I said.

"Certainly the last two," he said. "It's why we've talked about you and your mom having some kind of awareness to the stressors. Or maybe you have somebody who you create a relationship with, like a counselor or a psychotherapist, somebody who's skilled, who you meet with every week or every other week. It's about having someone who could be there for you and provide one more outlet."

"Yeah, I don't have a therapist." And my tone clearly indicated I didn't want one either.

"Well, you may want to consider that. A counselor could give you a little more to help offset those periods of stress."

I shrugged. I knew he was right, but fuck, it felt like I'd always be in some office talking about the same shit—my fucked-up mind.

"You'll still have your mom and your twin and your other siblings, but you may need a little more to try and combat the stress before, you know, you get to that point where that agitation comes out," he said.

I knew what he was referring to, and I instinctively pulled the sleeves down on my jacket. My right wrist still carried the scars from last summer.

"You know, like that reaction you had to your dad where it wasn't so much a self-injurious activity, but you did irritate your skin. That's how I think you explained it. It's a lot different than cutting or doing something like that, but it was a way for you to relieve stress, right? It was a reaction that you didn't think through," he said.

If I had thought it through, I would've brought a knife and I would've used it on the old man, not myself. Instead, when my dad and his girlfriend kept riding my ass about *every single thing* I did, I snapped. I went into the woods behind their house in Jackson, sharpened a stick as best as I could with a rock, and tried to end my life. There was no cutting for stress relief, there was only ending it all. The thought of lying on the valley floor surrounded by unending pine trees while I surrendered the fight calmed me.

Then Aaron found me and freaked out, and I blew it off as a bad high and skipping a dose of medication. But I wasn't stoned, and I hadn't even missed the hour I took my meds. The pressure was too great. The demands of my dad to be normal, to fit in, to be more like Aaron, was too much. I knew my dad loved me and wanted the best for me, but I would always be a disappointment to him. He'd miss me, maybe even mourn me, but then I would no longer be an embarrassment to him.

"It was a way for you to relieve that high stress when you lived with your dad over the summer," Blaze said, bringing me back to the here and now. "So, you want to try to do all those things to offset that. And it seems to me like you really are doing a good majority of those things. You look at all those key things, like the diet, the exercise, your job, staying active socially, interacting with your family.

You have good relationships. You're successful at school."

Somehow the guy always knew how to help me see the best in a bad situation.

"Successful at school? That's a joke, right?"

"No. Now, I consider success because, really, you're doing as well as you chose to do at school. So that's considered a success. And we just talked about the job and fraternity. You're in a good environment. You're not living in the fraternity house or with your dad, you're in an apartment, so you're not in a crazy situation. You're really doing all the right things," he said.

The way Blaze summed it up, my life didn't seem so pathetic.

"And when you're doing all this, it's going to help you manage what's happening. The last time you were here, we put you on a new medication to help keep your sleep schedule more consistent. I was a little worried about your sleep pattern and the excessive amount of sleep you needed," he said, which I knew was my cue to speak.

"It's gotten better."

His entire body seemed to nod. "Okay."

He crossed his legs and interlaced his fingers. I half expected some yoga chant to follow.

"During our last session, you mentioned that your sleep schedule was interfering with school. You need to go to class, because that's kind of your job. I mean, if you think about it, school is sort of your job right now. It's not like you don't have other jobs with the fraternity and the parking department, but school, that's your main one."

I nodded. "Yeah, same lecture I get from my mom."

To anyone else, my comment would have sounded like a dick move, but with Blaze, I put as much as I could out there. I knew it didn't help me or anyone if I bullshitted my way through this and gave the expected answer. But there were still some truths I just wasn't ready to face, let alone voice.

"Lecture." Again he nodded. "I can see that. But since school is your main job, that's why we switched your medication. I don't want you to go to school all day and then go to bed at seven o'clock because you're tired. Social interaction is part of living, man."

"Agreed."

Blaze was such a trip, but he seemed to get me.

"So." He uncrossed his legs, and his interwoven hands followed suit. "How are the visual and auditory alterations?"

Blaze called them alterations. Dr. Cordova and Clive called them hallucinations. Semantics. It didn't matter what they were called, because if the medication did what every shrink I'd seen claimed, I'd never have to answer that question again. But my life was a series of medication medleys to find the "right balance." And I still wasn't sure they had.

"A couple of weeks ago, I was at home. My mom was clearing off the dinner table, and she leaned across me to get my silverware, but she had this knife in her hand, and it was aimed right at me." My palms started to sweat, so I wiped them on my thighs, which darkened the faded denim. "Anyway, I yelled at her because seeing that knife come at my throat is what the shadow people used to do and shit like that. So when it happens, and it hasn't happened in such a long time, it freaks me out."

Blaze rarely leaned forward in his chair, but he did at that point. "Okay. I want to make sure I understand this. When you saw your mom with the knife, it was something that had happened historically to you where you actually saw a visual presence of someone coming at you with something, like a knife."

"The knife, it's just characteristic of what the shadow people would do when I saw them. And it's usually stuff that's violent; they use knives, so it freaks me out when that stuff happens. It kind of throws me off. It's not like… I mean, I *know* I'm not seeing something, but it freaks me out, just the thought of that happening again." *I never want the shadow people or Trevor to return.*

"You haven't had those thoughts in a while, have you?" he asked.

"No. God, no." As far as I knew, Trevor was gone.

"Your reaction at the dinner table, that's more of a different kind of reaction. Let's just call it hypervigilance. Since you've experienced those episodes previously, you're more vigilant and more aware. So when you see something like that, it's a trigger, and you kind of react."

"And that's normal?" I asked when my real question was buried much deeper. *I'm not losing my mind again, am I?*

"Branson, what happened is *not* a reaction related to schizoaffective. It's really more of a response to seeing the knife and what it's represented in the past for you, which isn't unusual. Again, it's more hypervigilance on your part because you've had these episodes where the shadow people appear with knives, so you're very keen to those situations and respond," he said.

"So it's kind of like PTSD," I surmised.

"PTSD is anxiety—extreme anxiety. What's happening with you is just part of where you're at now and how you react. When you become more conscious of the things that occur and realize it wasn't a hallucination, you'll see it as the reaction it was. And when you're more aware of these reactions, then you can control them." He leaned back against his chair.

"For instance," he continued, "if that were to ever happen again, you may be able to think back to that situation with your mom and be able to recognize that and not yell, jump, or startle. So you just add that to another experience you've had where you learn more and are able to control it better. It's sort of that top tier, where consciousness leads to control. The more conscious you are, the more you're able to control."

"Okay, I get that in theory, but...."

"Okay, so think of it like you're at a party and you're drinking too much. You have this conscious realization that you're drinking too much and no one else is drinking as heavily as you are, so you switch to water. That's where you want to get. It'll help you have better control. Your mind is very powerful and it reacts, so when these events occur, you want to be conscious of them so you have a better chance of control over them."

"Consciousness leads to control." It was the one thing that made sense.

"It takes practice. Day to day, month to month, year to year, it takes practice. Remember you've had these historical events that your mind can't control."

"When Trevor was in control," I said.

"Trevor was a symptom. So if you think of it like that, as a symptom, you'll regain the power of your mind. Your mind is doing things that you can't control when you've had these historical events with visual and auditory alterations. But with medication you *will* continue to have better control over them," he explained.

Neither Trevor nor the shadow people had surfaced in a really long time, so clearly something was working. At least I had that going for me.

"But like I said, Branson, I think you're doing a *really* good job. The things you're doing now, with school, the fraternity, living in your own apartment, and your continued social interactions, if you keep all those in your repertoire, it'll help during the difficult periods in your life."

"Okay, before you give me a gold star, I did come close to losing my shit on this girl today. She was talking some shit about me, or actually what I did in the past." I thought about the sorority girl and her comments. "I didn't key off, but there was a part of me that wanted to snap her head off."

That'd shut her down.

I shook my head. "Anyway, the only reason I *didn't* was because I needed something from her." *Maybe I'm not making progress.* I slunk farther into the couch. "So basically, I manipulated her to get what I wanted." I rolled my eyes. "I sank to her level."

"Branson, remember that guilt will tell you you've done something wrong while shame tells you you *are* wrong. You're shaming yourself, and shame has no place in your recovery."

I was expecting a "man" to follow that statement and was a little shocked that it didn't. The guy was a trip, but he really seemed to care, at least.

"I get what you're saying, but I just didn't fit in. I knew it, *she* knew it, and she made sure everyone *else* knew it, and it was pretty sucky. I felt like the third monkey fighting to get on Noah's ark."

His laughter wasn't like Clive's or Dr. Cordova's, but it had its own flair that made me smile.

"Branson, everyone has those days. I have to attend annual medical conferences, and I walk in feeling like an imposter. That's just life, man."

With all his degrees mounted on the wall, it was hard for me to imagine that Blaze wouldn't fit in anywhere. But I also doubted that he'd lie just to make me feel better about myself. Shrinks just didn't do that. They were painfully honest.

"That's why you want to keep going down the path with school, the fraternity, and your social interactions. Your stress doesn't get any less, so when those things build, like what happened at your dad's house or with this girl, it's called stress responses. Your body's built you up to it. You were so keyed off and frustrated, your body was leading you down this natural path. And on top of it, you have other things you have to deal with," he said.

"Yeah, she was horrible," I chimed in.

"Horrible is an extreme. That's one of those extremes. And your body will react to your mind, like at your dad's." Again he leaned forward, but this time he made direct eye contact with me. "Branson, I know from our sessions that what you did at your dad's wasn't the path you want to go down. And you won't have to have that response again where you take the hurt out on yourself. You have more control today."

Hurt. There were too many hurts to consider.

"There are people in this world who do things that you don't appreciate, like this girl—and who wouldn't be irritated by that? But by framing it as horrible, what happens is that your body starts to react to that event as being horrible, so if it happens again, your body gears up for that eventuality."

"So just one word, like 'horrible,' can trigger a reaction?" I asked.

"Horrible *is* an extreme. What you want to do is ask yourself what you can do to look at this situation factually. The only control you have is yourself. You can't control your mom, your brother, your dad, his girlfriend, or this girl. By looking at situations factually, you won't have these events that take you to this level that you regret, don't feel right about, or aren't able to come out of."

"Okay." I let go of the breath I was holding. "But when these things happen, they're just happening."

"Agreed. But anger and agitation are the same thing physiologically and cause the same reaction. So when you get out of whack, the stress responses come out, and eventually, if you don't manage that stress to help you cope with it, your body starts to break down, and then you can't handle other things that happen. Suddenly, you're not effective in school, in your social life, and all those other areas you're involved in. But if you did have someone in your life, someone you can talk to on a regular basis, it would help you become more conscious of your responses and reactions."

"Okay, let me see if I get this. We're *all* conditioned to have responses, right? But for me, it's how I process it that keeps Trevor and the shadow people at bay? And just by talking to someone, I'll have a better way to handle these stress reactors. I mean...." My shoulders tensed. "If controlling my response was all I had to do, then what's with all the meds?"

"Look at this situation factually, not emotionally. All of these events in life, if you think about them in the extremes—the girl was horrible, your dad is awful, his girlfriend is terrible—then your thought processes have the ability to impact you physically and psychologically. But if you look at these events factually, like 'I have schizoaffective disorder; I have this issue and ways to control it with medication and therapy,' then it doesn't have control *over* you," he said.

My hands flew out by my sides, speaking for me before I could form words. "I can't control *anything*—you just said that—so how the hell am I going to control this?"

"You're right. You don't know what's going to transpire over your lifetime, but it's how you want to think of things and where you want to be headed in life. Branson, how you frame what happens has tremendous impact over how your body responds. You do have the power to frame what happens by framing it factually and not emotionally. Remember, consciousness leads to control."

My shoulders surrendered into a shrug. "Okay."

"It's like how we factually *know* that diet and nutrition are key to healthy living. So when you eat well and exercise, your body responds. With your other issues, you take medication. And with the medicine, we factually know that you continue to get better control over your schizoaffective," he said.

I took a slow, steady breath. "I *do* factually know that life without medication sucks." I grinned. "Listen, there's no better way to frame it than 'sucks.' Life with meds isn't great, but it's better than how *horrible* it gets. And, Doc, we both know it gets horrible."

"Progress, that's all I'm suggesting. How you frame things sets your body up to respond."

Suddenly, I thought of my mom, and my throat practically closed. I swallowed, but the stronghold remained. When I finally spoke, my voice sounded rough. "My mom said she was tired of letting cancer win, so she started fighting and—" The thought made me smile. "—her body responded. She's now had *two* clean screens in a year."

His grin said it all. "That's great news. The power of how you frame events in your life *does* make a difference.

So, how are your little sister and brother?"

"They're good. I'm taking them all out to dinner tonight."

His face crinkled with a smile. "That's beautiful."

I laughed. "Yeah, it is."

"Okay, we won't make any new adjustments to your medications because it sounds like your sleep is balancing out. What about your depression?"

"It hasn't been an issue," I said, which was true.

He slowly nodded. "And you haven't had any side effects with your antidepressant?"

"No, not even weight gain on this dose."

"Excellent. Remember, staying active and social helps offset depression. Depression likes isolation. Don't feed it."

I chuckled. "When I work trail crew in the summer, there are always signs about not feeding the bears and wildlife."

Blaze grinned. "Branson, that's a good analogy and factually solid. Don't feed the bear."

"I won't."

He cupped his knees and stood, and I mirrored him. "Give your mom my best," he told me. "And have fun at dinner." He led me to the door.

"Will do."

Before I left his office, I did something I hadn't done with him. I extended my hand, which he shook. "Thanks."

"You're welcome, Branson. Look forward to seeing you next month."

CHAPTER 10

AARON

THE Cowboy Junkies played from the overhead speakers and echoed across the white cinder block walls. There was something sexy about the singer's voice. Her swoon-worthy take on an old Lou Reed song sounded like she was whispering in my ear. And damn if I didn't wish my name was Sweet Jane.

The more she sang, the more hushed the bar seemed to become. No one wanted to talk over the hauntingly romantic song. *Respect.*

I glanced around the dimly lit cave and spotted her behind the counter. Hannah. Her brown hair was tied in one of those messy buns that Carson once told me wasn't easy to make look messy. I could practically smell her from where I stood. I expected last night to be a simple hookup, but there was something about this one. Her face was angelic. And when she spoke my name, it was like God himself was calling me home. She was simply gorgeous.

But Hannah was more than just some sorority hottie. She was smart, funny, and fuck if she couldn't mix a drink.

I laughed. My heart had already overtaken my mind.

Would that be so bad?

The bar was open early in preparation for one of the last football games of the season. She was pouring a shot of whiskey into a hot cup of coffee for some frat guy, who leaned way too far over the bar for my taste. In a maroon sweatshirt with gold Greek letters across his chest, it was like he announced to the world that he bought his friends. It was the same thing I'd said to Branson when he joined a fraternity. *Lame.* I was a GDI—God Damn Independent—and proud of it. I didn't need some guy swatting my ass with a paddle while I recited the Greek alphabet to feel good about myself. Or that I belonged to something.

When she saw me, my stomach fluttered like it did before the start of a track event. My palms instantly got clammy, and I was pretty sure my upper lip had a sweat mustache going on.

Jesus. Get a grip, Aaron.

I cocked my head toward her like I was chill. Really, it was the only move that didn't require me to speak since I was pretty sure I'd sound like an idiot if I did.

"Hey, Aaron, what's your poison?" she said with a wink that about dropped me. This girl was trouble—in all the right ways.

I shrugged, still not sure my voice would work.

"Irish coffee? Mexican coffee? Perhaps a Bavarian?"

Her eyes danced, and I felt myself fall for a woman I

barely knew.

"Bavarian?" was all I said.

"Ah, yeah." Hannah slowly nodded, and her lips curved into a delicious smile. Those lips did things to me last night that I didn't think was humanly possible.

"So what's in it?" I asked, finally finding my voice.

"Peppermint schnapps, Kahlua, a dash of sugar, whipped cream, and my personal favorite, chocolate curls."

"So, this Bavarian drink." I raised an eyebrow, and she replied with a grin. "Does it have *any* coffee in it?"

Her cheeks instantly flushed. "Duh, of course, and coffee!"

Our laughter mixed like a blended, rich coffee that I couldn't wait to drink.

The moment was perfect. So of course it had to be ruined.

A group of her sorority sisters pulled a table across the granite floor, which was worse than nails on a chalkboard, the shock to my nerves continuing the longer they dragged it.

I pleasantly smiled in their direction as I darted to their rescue. The sooner I got there, the sooner I could return to the bar and to Hannah.

"And who are you?" A woman with white-blonde hair and dark roots tilted her ruby red lips into a smile.

"I'm Aaron. And you are?"

"Not interested," she said with a laugh as if she had coined the turndown.

"Well, that's good, because I'm here for Hannah." I pushed past her and grabbed the table. "Where you want it?"

"Uh, clueless much? In the corner with all the pink balloons." Her tone was as sharp as her pink stiletto-shaped nails that looked like they could tear into my skin as easily as her tone.

What's her problem?

Four other women dressed in pink shirts and jeans made their way toward us with Hannah not far behind.

"I see you've met our vice president," Hannah said when she reached me.

I nodded. "So breast cancer awareness? That's cool."

"Glad you approve of our philanthropic cause." The VP added an eye roll, and I wanted to slap the stink off her face. *What the fuck is her deal?* The only vice president I'd hated simply on principle was Wyoming-proud Dick Cheney, but this chick was a very close second.

"So, is there anything else I can help with?" I directed my question toward Hannah, but it was the vice president who spoke. With that white-blonde hair, she kind of reminded me of Cheney's oldest daughter, Liz, who was no picnic either. But hey, Liz prayed for us nonbelievers, so at least I had that going for me.

"Well...." The sorority girl heavily exhaled through her mouth. "There're two boxes in the trunk of my car that we still need, if you think you can handle it. They're pretty heavy." She eyed my arms. I knew I hadn't worked out in a while, but I didn't think I had lost that much muscle mass. Or had I?

"I've got it," I said with sinking confidence.

"You sure? Your arms look like buggy whips," she said,

which everyone laughed at, including me.

"Yes," I said in a kinder voice than I felt like using. "Point me toward your car."

"Well, Buggy Boy, it's the only silver Range Rover with pink trim in the lot."

Really? A nickname? I relaxed my hands lest they turn into fists. *This woman.* She acted with the arrogance and mean-spiritedness of Cheney, but with her black roots and bleached hair, she suddenly reminded me of Cruella de Vil. And I wasn't a fan.

Still, when she tossed me her shimmery pink keys, I snatched them midair with a knowing grin. *Yeah, who's got buggy whips now?*

She didn't seem to care, too busy bossing her underlings around.

"Hannah, we're going to need more balloons," she said.

"No problem. After my shift ends, I'll pick up another dozen."

That's my Hannah. I practically beamed beside her. She just made everything better.

"Oh." The VP purposefully paused. "That's right, you *have* to work."

What the fuck? I knew Jefferson Heights had a class discrepancy between those who had and those who didn't. I just didn't realize the haves and have-nots extended to insulting my girl. *You have to work? What the fuck is that? Yeah, most of us work.*

The VP's disinterest in anyone other than herself was really annoying. Her arrogance was disgusting. And the way Hannah seemed glued to her every word took my anger to an entirely new level. *Why doesn't she see through her?*

"Buggy Arms, what are you waiting for, an invitation? We need those boxes." The VP glanced at Hannah. "Are you *sure* about this one?"

And again, everyone laughed—including Hannah.

CHAPTER 11

AARON

LONELINESS clung to me and weighed me down with thoughts of home. I didn't want to be alone, but I couldn't stay with Hannah, not while that sorority bitch was there. I left the bar and wandered toward my apartment.

Branson was right. Moving away from Wyoming was a mistake. I knew no one, and anyone I did meet was an asshole. Hannah had been the exception. And now that was ruined.

Fuck.

I need a dog.

I grabbed my phone and searched online for the nearest animal shelter. A few popped up: Cat's Meow, Rescue Bark, and Pups n' Pussies.

"Pups n' Pussies?" I laughed, and a dark-haired girl who lived in the adjoining apartment complex stared at me strangely. "That's the name of a dog shelter—Pups n' Pussies."

My explanation had zero effect. People back east had no sense of humor. *Whatever. She's probably friends with that sorority VP.*

I hit the link for Pups n' Pussies, and within seconds, walking directions to the shelter materialized on my phone. I pulled up the hood on my navy sweatshirt and buttoned my gray peacoat that served as an added outer layer, and my mood instantly improved.

I wore clothes well. My dad's girlfriend called him a clotheshorse, and so was I. Actually, I was more of a clothes whore. Didn't matter if I had the money; when I found a style that looked good on me, I bought it. My credit card was practically maxed, but I didn't care. If a men's clothing store were to suddenly pop up before me, I'd open a line of credit and go ham.

Instead, brick buildings blurred past me. I turned left at the residential apartments and walked north, following the red blip on my phone. I didn't know how my mom or dad survived without cell phones. They both talked about some Thomas Guide map shit, highlighting routes in yellow and learning to navigate without Siri or Google Maps. *Insane.*

I caught my reflection in the sheet of windows that framed the red-bricked student cafeteria. Even with the hood pulled up, my jeans, boots, and jacket looked effortlessly hip. My dad definitely taught me how to dress, if nothing else.

"Own the clothes, don't let them own you," he told me. "And don't pollute the air with some shitty cologne. One spray of the good stuff in the center of your chest is enough."

I remember Branson laughing and elbowing my dad at that.

"What chest? This is Aaron you're talking about."

Asshole.

The memory made me grin and feel less lonely. *Maybe I should just hop on a plane and go home.* I knew Branson would be there. There was rarely a weekend that he stayed at his apartment in Casper. Besides, I could miss Monday classes.

I paused on the outskirts of campus and considered my options. Walk to the animal shelter and hope to find a rescue that was right for me, or book a flight and have a boarding pass ready to scan my way back to Wyoming?

I scrolled through the flight options, which was infinitely easier than choosing my next best friend. Shit, for less than three hundred bucks, I could leave in an hour and be in Wyoming by dinnertime.

My finger lingered over the Purchase button when my phone vibrated in my hand.

Branson.

"Hey, bro, I was just thinking of you," I said.

The only sound I heard was my brother's sobs.

"Bran, what's wrong?"

I heard him clear his throat, but he still didn't speak.

"What's going on? Talk to me." *Is Trevor back?* My vision blurred, and I lost all sense of where I was. I glanced around, but nothing looked familiar. "Come on, Branson, talk to me."

"It's Mom."

Like taking a punch to the gut, I folded into the pain that seared me. *Please no. Please don't tell me she died.* I couldn't catch my breath. *Not Mom. Please, God, not Mom.*

I staggered to the closest building and leaned against it. When my legs could no longer hold me, I slid down the side.

"What happened?" Tears streamed down my face.

"She's…."

"Is she dead?" The words sounded foreign, like someone else had said them. My body shook. *I'm all alone.*

"No. God, no."

I tucked my chin to my chest and cried. For a solid minute, I cried into the collar of my hoodie. *Mom, please don't ever leave me. I'll be better, I promise.* Just the thought of my mom dying ripped me in half. I couldn't stop crying because I couldn't imagine a worse loss.

"Aaron? Aaron, you still there?"

I couldn't talk.

"God, I'm sorry. She's alive. She's just…."

My strength was gone. My ability to handle shit and know how to deal with it no longer functioned. I felt broken, truly and utterly shattered.

"What? What, Branson!" I snapped. "What's wrong with Mom?"

"It's the cancer. It spread to her ovaries."

I shook my head. "No, you're *fuckin'* wrong. She just started a new job. And she passed her second mammogram. She told me. She wouldn't lie to me." *Would she?*

"She did. But…."

"But what? What the fuck, Branson!"

"She was having some pain, so they did this MRI where

I guess they look at everything, not just her breast cancer, and that's when they noticed some spots on her—"

"No! You're wrong. Mom doesn't even have ovaries. After Jack was born, she had all that taken care of."

"Bro, she told me she had her tubes tied, but she still has ovaries. That's why she's going to have that surgery where they remove everything."

"Will that fix it?" The air had turned, and the slab of concrete I sat on next to the building was freezing. I shivered and then couldn't stop my teeth from chattering. "Branson, will the surgery fix her?"

"That's the thought."

"That's the thought? What the fuck? Will it or won't it fix her?" My tone was as harsh and as constant as the back-and-forth wind that slapped me in the face.

"Jesus, I don't know. How the fuck would I know?" His outburst was followed by a long pause. And in that moment, I felt every emotion in his silence. "Aaron... I don't know."

Something clicked inside me that heard what my brother wasn't saying.

He needs me, not my anger or fear. He needs me to be the strong one, the brave one, the twin who holds him up.

So I lied.

"Bran, it's going to be okay."

He cleared his throat, and I swallowed thickly.

"I'm coming home," I said.

"What?" His confusion was palpable.

"I was seconds away from buying a ticket and surprising you guys when you called."

"Really?"

"Hundred percent." I wiped my nose on the shoulder of my jacket. "I thought it was one of those twin things when you called, like you knew."

"Nah, bro, I didn't. Are you *really* coming home?"

Home. I didn't even know where that was anymore.

"Yeah. Hold up." I glanced at the screen on my phone and blinked until the airline app came into focus. The next flight was in less than an hour. I'd never make it. But there was another one that left at four. I'd be home in time for dessert.

"I'm booking it now," I told him while I clicked my way through the transaction. "Done." I pressed the phone against my ear. "Pick me up at Cheyenne Airport at seven."

"I'll be there."

I was about to hang up when Branson called my name.

"Yeah?"

"Thanks."

I bit the inside of my cheek to stop from crying again. "Thank me by being on time."

His laughter was unlike the girls' in the bar. His raised me up rather than raising my hackles.

"I'll be on time. Do you want me to tell Mom?"

I shook my head. "No. Let it be a surprise. A good surprise, I hope."

"Bro, you've always been Mom's favorite."

Now I laughed. "Sell that shit to someone who'll believe it. Listen, I've gotta go pack a bag. I'll see you in Cheyenne at seven."

CHAPTER 12

AARON

THERE was only one airport in Cheyenne, which was tucked behind the Catholic cemetery. It was creepy as shit, but it was less than two miles away from my mom's house. So even though the Cheyenne airport only flew into Dallas/Fort Worth, which meant routing my flight from Ohio to DFW and then hopping on a little puddle jumper to get to Cheyenne, I did. The upside was that as soon as I departed the plane and stepped foot on Wyoming soil, I'd be home in under five minutes.

Home.

Adrenaline spiked through me as I walked from the tarmac into the terminal. It felt like Christmas morning. And the best present stood off to the side with his hands in the front pockets of his jeans like he didn't know what to do with them. I heard our dad's voice: "Pockets are for change, not pool." My dad was so concerned with how things looked, and playing pocket pool with our junk definitely topped the list of what we shouldn't do.

I didn't care what either of our parents said. Neither of their voices was as strong to me as my brother's. I walked toward him, and my chest suddenly betrayed me by shaking. When I reached Branson, I dropped my overnight bag and wrapped my arms around him. I didn't know who held the other tighter, only that we weren't going to let go.

Home.

It didn't matter the shape I was in, or the fact that my hands shook and I probably smelled rank from running back to my apartment to pack. Branson would always take me in. He would always be there for me. And I'd always be there for him.

"I'm so glad you're here." His voice reassured me that I'd done the right thing by flying in.

I nodded against him. "You really freaked me out."

"Bro." Branson patted my back before he released me. "I'm sorry about that."

I shrugged.

"Did you think—" Branson looked around and then lowered his voice. "Did you think Trevor was back or something?"

"Yeah." My tone was a bit edgier than I intended. "I mean, do you blame me?"

When Branson smiled, his eyes practically disappeared. I was sure the same thing happened to me, but it wasn't like I looked at myself when I smiled.

"You're an idiot," I said, and he laughed.

"True." He glanced behind me. "Do you have any

checked bags?"

"Nah, this is it." I grabbed my bag off the floor and walked beside my brother toward the car. "She has no idea, right?"

"Not a clue."

When Branson opened the door, my senses were already primed. My mom always made sure the house looked and smelled good, and I inhaled an inviting scent of cinnamon and vanilla that swirled lightly through the air like a warm embrace. My mom's go-to scented candle was on the fireplace mantle, the flicker of the flame welcoming me home.

But as I stepped across the threshold, there was another smell that almost overpowered the candle. A strong, acidic, pine-scented ammonia burned my nose.

"What the…?" I waved a hand in front of my face.

Branson curtly shook his head like a warning and lowered his voice. "Mom still gets sick—a lot. It's to cover the smell of puke."

I stood in the foyer and stared at the candle's flame. My mom's candles could mask anything—her failed cooking attempts, the pot that Branson and I smoked in high school, our rancid football cleats. *When did it stop working?*

My bag fell off my shoulder to the floor with a thud.

"Who's home?"

Her voice in the distance made my eyes water and my throat tighten.

Mom.

Branson elbowed me.

"It's me, Mom," I said but didn't move.

The next sound I heard was the rapid rhythm of her feet on the hardwood floors. Tears fell down my cheeks. I tried to wipe them away, but suddenly someone who faintly looked like my mom appeared in the living room. My chest felt heavy and my legs wouldn't move, though I wasn't sure they'd hold me up anyway.

It was hard to see your icons, your heroes, have a weakness. At a solid five foot one, my mom was someone who was about as intimidating as a one-month-old German shepherd, but she always had one helluva bite. Any time anyone messed with any of her kids, my mom came out fighting. Tara Louise Lafontisee cared more about her children's happiness than her own.

And now....

"Aaron?"

The knot in my throat felt like it was going to choke me.

My beautiful mom suddenly looked small and frail. Branson told me she didn't look good, but I wasn't prepared for just *how* different she looked. Granted, I hadn't been home in almost a year, but how was this possible? Patches of red hair matted her head, and her normally healthy, full face had been replaced with sunken cheeks and deep, dark crevices under her green eyes. It was like someone had pulled a plug and drained the life out of her.

"How did you get here?" She looked from Branson to me. "Did you fly?"

I could only nod, because I realized the knot in my throat was my heart.

She touched the top of her head. "It'll grow back," she said as if reading my thoughts.

I didn't know what to say or do. *Mom. Oh, Mom.*

"If I had known you were coming, I would have...." She tucked a wisp of hair behind her ear and broke eye contact with me. "I don't know, put on something nicer." She was in a white thermal and charcoal-colored leggings that barely clung to her and sagged around her ankles.

"Are you kidding?" Carson walked into the foyer with the grace and poise of a seasoned dancer taking the stage. She gently rubbed our mom's nearly bald head. "Mom's a straight-up fox."

My sister's green catlike eyes fell on me. "Uh, hello?"

"Hey, sis." My shock gave way to the reality that I was staring at my mom and my face most likely revealed everything I couldn't seem to say.

Why didn't Carson call me? Why didn't she tell me how bad things were? Don't they think I care?

I shook my head to snap out of the self-pity that suddenly consumed me when my mom walked toward me.

"Baby, it's okay." When she reached up and touched the side of my face, everything I'd kept so carefully safeguarded broke open.

"Branson said you passed the last two mammograms."

"I did," she said with a weak smile.

"Then...." I didn't know how to ask my mom why she looked like death.

"My oncologist put me on an oral chemo medicine, which is an upgrade from being hooked to a chemo drip, *but* it seems to have the same effect." She gently touched her head, and I felt like I'd break in two.

I gently wrapped my arms around her, but it was her arms that held me while I cried.

When did this happen? Why didn't you tell me?

She slowly exhaled. "I never thought a once-a-day pill could make me look and feel as awful as the chemo drip, but"—she shrugged—"it is what it is."

"You're going to be okay, right?" I said in my mom's ear.

But instead of telling me what I wanted to hear, what I longed to hear, what I *needed* to hear, she shook her head against me.

"I don't know," she admitted.

I pulled away from her and wiped my nose with my hand. "Ma, you're going to get through this."

"That's the plan." Carson draped a protective arm around our mom's shoulders and began to lead her away from me. "Mom's a badass." She glanced in my direction—glared, really. "But even badasses need to rest."

My mom rolled her eyes. "Oh, Carson, I'm fine. Your brother's home. I can rest when I'm dead."

The morbidity of her comment made me laugh.

"Jesus, Mom," Branson said, which made her smile. She always smiled at Branson.

I quickly looked around the living room. "Where's Jack?"

"He's at a birthday party sleepover," my mom said

before quickly switching gears. "I bet you're hungry."

I shrugged. "I could eat."

"Good thing we still have leftovers," Carson said over her shoulder as she led us toward the kitchen. "Branson took us all out to dinner."

"That's cool." *I flew from Ohio to Wyoming, but who's keeping track?*

The behemoth table was positioned in the center of the dining room and took up the entire space. It was the first piece of furniture my mom bought after her second divorce. It really wasn't much to look at, just a long chunk of oak with pointy edges that hurt like fuck whenever I ran into one, but to my mom, it was everything. It was a mammoth pain in the ass for Branson and me to move whenever Mom got an idea to change the ergonomics of the room, but that was when we'd lived in Casper. In this old house in Cheyenne, once the table was centered under the overhead light, it stayed.

My mom insisted we all eat at least one meal a week at this table together. It was where she'd celebrated all our birthdays and left treats for us to find after school. It was where she'd told us about Branson's diagnosis and the loss of her job.

I spent four years of high school with my ass parked at that table. Branson barely warmed a seat, but every night and on weekends, I sat with my laptop, my textbooks held open by yellow highlighters, and a stack of index cards beside me. It was the only way I absorbed all the crap that was thrown at me on a regular basis. From AP chemistry to

AP geometry, index cards kept me solidly on the honor roll for four straight years.

Now it seemed like I barely cracked a book. College was infinitely easier. Or maybe after everything I'd dealt with in high school, my retention rate was gone. Besides, the crap the professors doled out no longer mattered. Or did it ever? At the end of the day, the most important things in life didn't happen in a lecture hall, in a textbook, or on an index card but around this table. That was all I needed.

Now the table had tubs of colored paint, plastic gloves, poster boards, yellow yarn, and rolls of colored duct tape scattered across it.

"Your sister is running for school senate," my mom said as way of explanation. "I'm so proud of her."

She reached toward the pile, and her ribs showed through her thermal top. *Jesus, Branson, you said she lost weight, not that Mom looked like a skeleton. What kind of fucked-up chemo pill do they have her on?*

"Ma, I got it." I quickly scooped the craft supplies with my arm and pushed everything to the far end of the table—hospital-grade gloves and all.

The heart of our home brought this table into our lives and created a safe space for us. Caught up in the moment, I wrapped my arms around her.

"Love you, Mom."

She leaned her head against my shoulder, and I gently rested my chin on the top of her balding head. The floral scent of her perfume brought me back to my childhood, when the biggest worry I had was how to build the next Star

Wars Lego set. A mix of emotions turned me inside out, but I vowed to hold it together for her sake. I was the strong one, after all. Always had been, always would be.

"You didn't need to come home." She patted my arm. "But I'm so happy you're here."

Her optimism couldn't raise my sunken heart. It was clear from her weight loss that her nausea was constant, her hair was mere wisps at this point, and worst of all, Tara Lafontisee seemed weakened. Like watching Superman being slowly tainted by kryptonite, my mom was slowly becoming less of the strong figure I had once known. My hero was fading away in front of me.

Make it stop.

It was easily the hardest part of cancer from the point of an outsider, watching someone you loved show signs of weakness. Sure, my mom had the occasional emotional breakdowns when I was growing up, but she was always impenetrable. Nothing stopped her. Ex-husbands, her past, publishers who didn't want a sequel to her book on education—none of that mattered, because nothing prevented my mom from moving forward. But now... she not only looked frail, she *was*. Cancer not only slowed her down, it seemed determined to win.

I kissed the top of her head, wishing I could kiss away the pain the way she had done for me countless times.

Please don't die.

Branson held a chair out for her, but before she sat down, she hugged my brother.

"Thank you," she said to my other half. My mom was

always the great equalizer. If she hugged one of us, she made sure to hug the rest of us.

Carson took charge in the kitchen with the leftovers. So much had changed since I left. Carson was no longer the little middle schooler I remembered. She was now in high school and clearly didn't take shit from anyone, whether it was cancer or an absent, clueless older brother. Carson was a mini version of our mom *before* cancer.

That's a trip. When did our life move from before to after cancer? I knew the timeline, but my heart still couldn't make sense of it. The "before" part I got, but "after"? The "after" portion seemed to keep being pushed further and further back. Then again, was there ever really an "after" to cancer?

All I knew was that my mom was fading away, and there was nothing I could do to stop the progression.

When she sat down, Branson took a seat on one side of her and I took my place on the other side. Carson did what my mom would have done in the past, busying herself in the kitchen, making sure we all had something to eat.

"So…." My mom placed her hands on the table in front of her. Veins crisscrossed her pale, tissue paper–like skin. "I'm thinking Branson or one of your siblings told you about the call from my surgeon."

"Uh, kind of," I said. "I really don't know the details. I just knew I needed to be here."

She reached across the table and took my hand.

"Oh, Aaron." Her green eyes brimmed with tears, and I gritted my teeth. I couldn't keep breaking down like a blubbering idiot. *She needs me to be strong*.

I cleared my throat. "So, what *is* happening?"

"Well, I was in some discomfort, so I had an MRI, which is when they saw this spot on my right ovary. My surgeon called because they were concerned with it." She squeezed my hand. "They took a biopsy of it and…." She shrugged. "Damnedest thing, it came back as a low-grade malignant tumor."

"Malignant." The word made me shiver. One fucking word that held so much power and despair. *How could this happen again?*

It was August 20th when my brother and I got the email. After my mom lost her job at the university, the community college in Cheyenne offered her a teaching job. I assumed the email was about her upcoming class.

Boys, my students will find out about this on Monday, but you're not my students, you're my sons. My doctor called today, and I have ductal carcinoma, which is a form of breast cancer.

My mother, a woman who went through years of abuse and two divorces, now diagnosed with cancer. Reading her email was the hardest thing I'd ever done. Even harder than finding out my twin brother was diagnosed with schizoaffective disorder. At least when Trevor tried to take over my brother's thoughts, I felt like there was someone to fight.

But ductal carcinoma? Cancer? How did you fight that? Tara Lafontisee was this unstoppable woman with no weaknesses, and to hear there may be a flaw to this perfect person stopped me on a dime. It was unbearably hard to hear that word used to describe an inherent flaw I had overlooked. Her email focused on the upside of the cancer—as if there was one. But my mom was good with the spin. She spun her diagnosis like it was a minor blip on the radar. She told us the cancer was in her milk ducts and hadn't spread, which was all positive.

Still, cancer? It was the one word I wouldn't have associated with my mom, ever. And I never thought there was another word in the English language that would hold such power over me until now.

Malignant.

When it was ductal carcinoma, it was all I thought about for months. It consumed me. I was a sophomore in college at the time, and I tried to think of ways to make my mom's life easier so she could focus on herself for once. I applied to be a resident advisor in the dorms, which would cover most of my living expenses in college. But I bombed the interview, so that hope was shot to the ground. I worked at a fast-food chain on campus to pay for textbooks, but I still ended up overdrawing my account. For some stupid reason, I stopped keeping track of what I earned compared to what I spent and ended up with a negative balance. My mom had done so much for me, and when it was my turn to return the favor, I shit the bed. Nothing I did to help ended the way I anticipated; I only created more stress in her life. The more attempts I made, the worse I seemed to make things for her.

I couldn't do that to her again, but I didn't know what to do to make things better. I wanted to take the cancer from her and put it on myself. But what I wanted even more than that was to be held by my mom and told everything was going to be all right.

I bit the inside of my cheek to stop from crying.

"Does it hurt?" I asked.

She tried to smile away my question, but I knew.

"Ma?"

Her eyes glistened, and she barely nodded. "It feels like bad cramps," she said finally.

"Mom, who are you kidding?" Carson stood in the kitchen and shook her head. "Cramps don't make you double over and almost pass out." She glanced at Branson and then me. "She's in a lot of pain on a pretty frequent basis."

My mom said nothing to refute my sister.

What the fuck? Why didn't anyone tell me? Just because I live in Ohio doesn't mean I don't care.

"When did this happen?" I heard the defensiveness in my voice. "No one told me you were still in pain."

"Sweetheart, I told your sister and brother not to bother you with this when you're so far away. *And* this happened so suddenly that we thought it might be a reaction to the oral chemo, so there was nothing to tell you until we knew more."

"So what are they going to do?" I asked when what I should have asked was how I could help.

"My oncologist and surgeon both agree that a total hysterectomy is the best course of action. They'll remove everything—the uterus, ovaries, and fallopian tubes, which will also remove all the visible cancer."

"Visible? What about what they can't see?" I asked.

"That's a very good question," she said, and despite myself, I smiled. My mom was the consummate educator. "After the surgery, I'll start another round of chemo, and they'll take me off the oral chemo, which may just be a good thing." Her voice was upbeat, but the fight was gone from her eyes.

There's no upside, no spin, is there, Ma? The cancer, which wasn't supposed to spread, had. The ache in my body felt like I was being split in two. *How much longer will you be here? How much time do I have left with you?*

"What stage is it?" My voice was barely recognizable.

When her lip trembled, I had to look away or I'd lose it. And I couldn't do that to her. I couldn't be a burden. I had to keep it together. I wouldn't let her down.

"We got lucky. It's only at stage one, but with my history...." She swallowed. "Well, that's why they've prescribed such an aggressive postsurgical treatment. You know, to ensure we get everything."

"But then it's done, right?" Branson said.

My mom gently smiled. "That's the idea."

I couldn't stop thinking of all she'd already been through. Years of physical and mental abuse from my father, followed by a shit show of a second marriage, and now this? The next thought came out of my mouth unbidden. "It's not fair."

She shifted her attention to me. No one's eyes had as much impact on my life as hers.

"Sweet boy, it is what it is."

"No." I shook my head. "That's bullshit. You don't deserve this."

"Shit, brother, if we got what we deserved, I'd be in Hell right now," Branson said.

My mom redirected the conversation off malignant ovarian tumors, surgery, and chemo to my twin.

"No," she said in *that* tone. It was the tone my mom had when shit was about to get real.

Ah, damn. Branson stepped in it.

"Do you think someone who has diabetes deserves to be in Hell?" she asked.

Branson raised his shoulders. "What?"

"Diabetes is a disease, and schizoaffective disorder is a mental illness. You have no more control over that than someone with diabetes."

Branson's hair, always so much shaggier than mine, flowed back and forth like a surfer as he shook his head. "Mom, it's not the same. A diabetic doesn't hide their symptoms or hurt the people they love."

My mom was the most unstoppable woman I knew. She didn't take shit from anyone, and God help the poor bastard who pointed out a flaw in her kids—even if it was one of her kids doing the pointing.

"Branson—" Her voice cracked and her lip trembled. "Please." She quickly wiped away a tear and straightened her posture as if the gesture would realign her emotions. "You're not *that* person. He's gone."

Trevor. *Fuckin' Trevor.* If I never heard that name again, it'd be too soon.

"It's okay, Mom," Branson said. "I'm not Trevor, but sometimes…."

"What?" I jumped in.

Branson shrugged. "Listen, you guys know that Trevor was part of my break from reality, but other people don't realize that and aren't as understanding." He waved his hand like it was nothing, but I knew from the way he wouldn't look at me that it meant something.

"Like who?" Carson stepped into the conversation.

"Oh, just this girl I met at the Albany campus fundraiser," he said.

"Albany Community College?" I asked. "Where we used to play club soccer?"

Branson nodded.

"What'd this girl do?"

"I went to this sorority fundraiser, and she was in charge." He shrugged. "This girl remembered me from high school, that party…." He briefly made eye contact with me.

There was only one party in high school where Trevor directed Branson.

"With Dakota?" I said, and again he nodded. "Yeah, that wasn't your best night, but Trevor was commanding the conversation. You can't let *one person's* opinion of you get to you."

"Dick." My twin brother looked at me.

"Exactly my point." I laughed.

"Fuck you," Branson said with a grin.

"Okay, enough of the fucking dick," Mom chimed in.

"That's what she said," Carson said, which caused us all

to burst out laughing.

The sound was such a welcome relief to the heaviness that hung in the room. By its very definition, cancer was a disease that divided, from cells in the body to the families it affected. For a brief moment, our collective laughter stopped that division.

But only briefly.

When the laughter died down, Branson nodded toward the rocking chair in the front room. "I did get the shirts I wanted. You see the ones I got for me and Mom?"

"The neon pink? Bro, couldn't miss it," I said, matching his grin.

He rubbed the stubble on his chin. "Hey, I put up with a real skank in a shitty wannabe college bar to get those shirts."

"I bet" was all I said. My own run-in with the VP of Hannah's sorority was enough to leave a bad taste in my mouth that I didn't want to revisit. I didn't know if I'd ever forget her "buggy boy" dig.

"Bran, want me to fight her?" Carson dropped a plate of reheated potato skins in the center of the table and wiped her hands on the towel draped over her shoulder. "I could take her, right?"

I thought of that sorority girl in Ohio who made fun of me, and suddenly I saw the humor in the moment. I raised an eyebrow toward my sister. "Shit, Carson, with those buggy-whip arms, you couldn't swat a fly. Hell, we might as well send little Jack."

If laughter actually *was* the best medicine, my mom

wouldn't need another surgery. But she did. And nothing I could say or do would cure her.

I wanted to act as if nothing was wrong, so I smiled. But despite what I showed my family, I felt myself sinking, and I couldn't find my way out of the darkness.

CHAPTER 13

DAVID AND ME

YOU'VE heard the stories. When someone has a choice between good or bad, they talk about the angel and devil sitting on their shoulders or leaning over to whisper in their ear.

The angel is always very clear.

"Johnny, if you take the last cookie, then your sister, Sally, who hasn't had one, won't get one."

The devil is a little more persuasive.

"Johnny, what's the harm in one cookie? Your sister's trying to lose weight. She'll thank you."

The line seems obvious. Take the cookie and you're a bastard; don't take the cookie and be the hero.

I was never one to be the hero in my own story.

"How dull is that?"

Agreed. Heroes were overrated.

On *Breaking Bad*, everyone rooted for Walter White, the chem teacher with cancer who was just trying to take care of his family. He turned to making meth to pay the bills.

"Was it really his fault that he became the main drug lord? Sure, some of his actions were questionable, like letting his partner's girlfriend OD, but the ends always justified the means."

Hundred percent.

Everyone wanted to be the antihero. It was cool. No one wanted to be the boring guy who got killed.

Besides, when it came down to it, the angel in my head fell a long time ago.

It was why I moved so easily between sanity and whacked. I had a sense of purpose. There was no angel or devil in my ear, only David.

And because I allowed David and myself brief periods of pure madness, I fortified my mind against the inner darkness that was a constant threat.

And tonight the darkness was real.

But through trial and error, I found that the key to living with schizophrenia was not voicing any troubles to the world—and certainly not to family. With everything they'd already been through and were going through, they would never understand. And they certainly wouldn't forgive. There was only so much forgiveness to go around, and schizophrenia made sure my portion was depleted. Schizophrenia was an equal opportunity offender—it fucked with the mind as much as it fucked with the family.

It was actually better that way. Everyone knew weakness was born in disclosure. Confessing was commonplace; the true test was keeping the darkness hidden, and so far, I'd passed the test brilliantly. In fact, I didn't think anyone else could've kept their symptoms hidden better than me. The key was not giving in to temptation.

It was way too simple in our modern, tech-driven, social media–heavy, me-saturated world to lose control to one's inner thoughts. Drinking made it even easier. And how many times did drunk texting ever work out?

"Uh, never."

Agreed.

I was smart. I had to be. I had to be smarter than my illness. Smarter than David. I already knew the downside to letting the voices take control—utter chaos. And worse, hurting loved ones. I wouldn't do that.

"I wouldn't want you to do that."

Understood.

Still, it was why I quietly made my exit from the basement and the Harry Potter movie marathon that Carson and my mom were engrossed in. My twin brother had already left to go check on some girl, which was what I needed to do as well.

Snagging a sweatshirt from the pile of clothes that my twin and I shared whenever we were home, I grabbed my backpack and loaded it with supplies. Everything I needed was within reach. I took a set of car keys off the hook and headed toward the car that beeped when I aimed the remote in its direction.

I slid into the driver seat, opened my laptop, and plugged the flash drive into the side. The only copy of my journal was stored on this drive. I didn't need to know what I typed when David spoke to me. Nor did I need anyone else to know. As soon as the journal entries were written and saved to the drive, I deleted the file from my laptop.

I didn't have any desire to discuss the entries with anyone because they only brought pain and sorrow. I was a great writer because I could fully express myself when I was at my weakest and most vulnerable. And that was when I allowed David to speak.

I sat in the car outside our house. Even with a new sweatshirt on, my mom's perfume clung to me like a distant memory. I inhaled deeply, and on the exhale, David spoke and I typed.

A Killer's Journal

Certain temptations and thoughts become stronger based on certain emotions that I feel through my life. When I'm angry, my mind instantly goes to cutting someone's jugular or strangling them with my hands.

When I'm sad, I think of more sadistic tendencies, like how to hurt someone for such a long period of time that they beg for their life to end. Excitement is more directed to the action of murder and watching the life drain out of a person's eyes. These emotions are what drove me throughout my adolescence. The idea of hurting or killing someone occupied my every thought.

As I got older, the reality that I could actually do it distracted me. Why should I have to work for money when I could just simply kill someone and take their wallet? Why do people try so hard to get by when the alternative is so much easier? I began to lose regard for human life and thought I was above everyone else. Anyone who wasn't me was simply a nuisance. That thought process disconnected me from everyone, and I no longer felt emotions like pity or jealousy. The only emotion that drove me was desire.

One thing I never disconnected from was my family. For some reason, hurting the ones closest to me crossed a line. Even the thought of hurting them made me sick. To this day, I have no idea why that was my line, but it was.

I was tired of typing, or rather transcribing David's thoughts as they bounced around my head like a stray bullet. It was time for action. I saved the file to the flash drive, shut my laptop, and set my sights on the fundraiser at Albany Community College.

Spiking her drink was so easy, it almost dulled me. And it came as no surprise that the sorority sister in charge of the event would still be by the bar manning the table while the rest of her pack played pool.

"Uh, I don't think you're supposed to wear those letters here." She pointed at my Greek sweatshirt.

"Bitch."

Yup.

I slid into the empty seat beside her. "It was all I could find that was clean." I sold the lie with a devil-may-care smile that seemed to do the trick.

"Well, as long as you know that *your* house isn't represented on *our* campus, I guess it's not *that* big a deal." She bumped her shoulder against mine.

"Is she flirting?"

Dunno. Don't care.

"Well, I wouldn't want to go and break the rules," I said.

"But you *are* a rule breaker, aren't you?"

"You have no idea."

I swallowed the laughter at the base of my throat and instead headed to the bar and ordered her another drink.

The more Fireballs she downed, the more I plied her cinnamon whiskey with the powder from crushed-up over-the-counter sleeping pills. I actually had my mom to thank for my ingenious idea. During one of our calls, I mentioned that my sleep cycles were off. Who knew she'd suggest a remedy that didn't require a prescription? Better yet, for less than five bucks, I could buy enough diphenhydramine to knock out a linebacker.

It was the best-kept secret on the drugstore shelf. I'd discovered that there were many over-the-counter sleeping pills that contained diphenhydramine, a powerful sedative that caused even the most stubborn insomniac like me to surrender to sleep. It was 100 percent legal and carried a bolded warning on the side of the box not to mix with alcohol.

"Oops."

I shrugged. Apparently too much of a good thing could cause innumerable problems, like liver or brain damage, alcohol poisoning, or even the risk of overdose. I didn't want to kill the skank, and I certainly didn't want to rape her. Oh no, she deserved so much more. I just had to ensure she didn't wake up prematurely. I had plans for her that required complete compliance.

Sprinkling the crushed tablets into her drink also safeguarded me against her remembering anything. The happy downside to diphenhydramine was that too much made a person foggy the next day. I'd learned that the hard way. It was like amnesia; I could barely remember my name, let alone what I'd done the previous night.

So while I knew she wouldn't need as much as I took when sleep evaded me, I had to balance it just right so she also wouldn't remember me or what I was about to do. After the third heavily laced shot, her face flushed and her eyelids began to droop. I swooped in.

"Hey, hey, looks like someone may have had one too many Fireballs," I said.

"Nah." She waved me away with her pink nails. "Gish me anover one."

I nodded. "No, I think you've had your quota." I glanced toward her sorority sisters, who were playing pool in the corner of the bar. From the way they kept scratching, it was clear they were too hammered to notice anyone leave, least of all this one. They hadn't paid attention to her since I showed up. The timing couldn't be better.

I swung her arm around my neck and tucked mine around her waist. When we stood, I balanced her to keep her from stumbling and led her to the door without a care in the world. Most people didn't see what was right in front of them.

"Refrigerator blindness at its best."

Agreed.

As I tucked her into the car, I held a bottled water with the last of the sleeping aid toward her before she passed out.

"Hey, you look dehydrated. Maybe some water?" I said.

She grabbed the water bottle like I had just offered her the fountain of youth. And maybe I had. One more sip would wash away her memory of tonight.

A full harvest moon hung low in the sky, providing the light I needed. I shifted her body over my shoulder and walked toward the end zone. Her head bounced against my back, which was kind of annoying. I tightened my hold on her legs, not wanting the girl to break her neck or anything. Not on my watch.

The football field was empty. It was a bye week, so there weren't any lights or cheering crowds. For a moment, I paused and glanced in the direction of the stands. It didn't matter what stadium or where it was located, my mom always sat in the same section—close to the fifty-yard line and roughly between rows ten and twenty. It was her thing, which was funny. She knew nothing about track or any field events, but she researched which were the best seats in a stadium. She didn't specify what sport, so I was sure it was for football, not track.

I would've laughed, but it just didn't seem right with this woman draped over my shoulder like the bag of trash she was. Still, for my mom's lack of understanding of track, she came to nearly every meet.

I imagined her long auburn hair split into two ponytails that were each tied with two different-colored ribbons—red and blue, one for me and one for my brother. I was red; he was blue. It was how she'd dressed us when we were little to tell us apart. *Red and blue and together we were the purplest.* My chest hurt at the memory. Or maybe it was the heels pressed against me.

"What happened? The mom you knew is all but gone."

You're probably right. She's going to let cancer win, isn't she?

Why? Why won't she fight? Mom, why won't you fight? We need you. I choked down the hurt. *I need you.*

"It's better she's not here." His voice grew stronger, a command to shut out the pain and look forward. *"This is the only way you'll be free. You need this."*

And just like that, I resigned myself to David's plan—whatever that was.

Her limp body grew heavy as I walked toward the tall, dark grove of hearty oaks surrounding the north end of the stadium. Thankfully the leaves hadn't fallen. I needed the coverage, the shelter.

What I was about to do wasn't for prying eyes.

When I finished, I stood back and surveyed our work.

"Not bad."

I probably went a bit too heavy on the eyes, but it was hard adding blue tempera paint to drooping eyelids with a foam paintbrush. But the bright pink paint that I used on her lips glided on much more smoothly and allowed me to extend her smile. She looked demented like the Joker, which wasn't the look I was going for, but this was a first for both of us.

Her inability to sit was really proving to be problematic. I couldn't carry her again because I'd get tempura paint all over me, and I'd worked too hard within the confines of the plastic gloves so I didn't leave any trace behind. I grabbed her arms and dragged her from the bushes and across the grass to the goalpost.

The post was covered in thick white vinyl foam padding. I knew this firsthand when I collided with the damn thing trying to protect the goal during our days playing club soccer. The thick padding was meant to reduce head injuries, but fuck if my cranium didn't hurt like hell afterward.

Still, it would give her something somewhat soft to lean against. I didn't want to hurt her, but I did want to humiliate her the way she liked to humiliate others.

"Something's missing."

I pulled her hair into two ponytails that I tied with yellow yarn. Now with the smeared paint and blonde ponytails, she looked like Harley Quinn.

"Fuck."

David's voice surfaced in my head.

"Why make her look good?"

His influence grew stronger, louder.

"Cut that shit off."

I rummaged through my backpack for my little brother's blunt-tipped scissors. They could barely cut construction paper, let alone hair.

"Cut."

David's voice was a command that shut out my ability to reason.

"Cut. Cut it off."

Too tired to fight, I put my thinking on autopilot and let David drive this train. I lifted one of her side ponytails and began to cut it with the scissors. I cut, and cut, and cut and then moved to the other side of her head. I cut until all that was left were two little stubs of white-blonde hair wrapped in yarn, poking out on the sides of her head.

"Isn't that better?"

I nodded.

"Don't forget the sign."

I draped another piece of yarn around her neck, which

was attached to a poster board that hung across her chest.

"Who's laughing now?" was written in red paint that dripped and made it look more menacing than I'd intended. David wanted it that way.

"Nice job."

I propped her up as best as I could against the foam padding, then quickly grabbed the duct tape from my backpack and began to wrap her to the post. I used the entire roll of neon green tape. I couldn't let her free herself until the entire Albany campus got a good look.

She wasn't going anywhere until some unlucky soul found her.

"Make no mistake. No one will rescue this girl. She's beyond rescuing. But someone may free her."

Agreed.

"You could leave her naked with just the sign."

But as soon as David suggested it, he changed his mind.

"Nah, that's going too far."

Agreed.

"We don't want to be cruel."

Agreed.

"Our work is done."

I stared at her duct-taped to the goalpost, and it all seemed like a dream. I mean, it wasn't *that* bad. Even my mom said hair grew back.

"So really, how much damage have we done?"

I didn't have an answer. My brain went blank.

I took a few pics with my phone before walking beneath the full moon that led me here.

CHAPTER 14

AARON

"IT'S taken me sixty-seven years to realize that hurting someone because I've been hurt by them doesn't work."

The priest leaned his elbows on the podium like he was addressing a locker room full of football players rather than a congregation dressed in their Sunday best.

"Trust me," he said, "I've tried all the workarounds. From convincing myself that I was simply giving the person a taste of their own medicine to the ever-popular quoting a verse out of scripture to justify my actions, nothing ever worked. Sure," he continued, cutting the air in front of him with his hand, "it temporarily relieved my conscience—but only temporarily."

Father Truman slowly made eye contact with each section of the church. I followed his gaze toward the choir loft where kids Jack's age sat beside the *Phantom of the Opera*-type pipe organ. The organist was hidden, which made it even more Phantom-like. My focus turned to the domed ceiling in the cathedral. Oak trim offset the cream-colored dome that was sprinkled with blue- and gold-painted stars. It was like looking straight into heaven, or at least what I imagined heaven looked like.

"Sanctus, Sanctus, Sanctus" was etched along the base of the ceiling. No matter how many times we went to mass, I always translated the Latin into English: "Holy, holy, holy."

"The temptation to act on how we feel is, well, tempting." Father Truman smiled and turned his attention to the pews opposite us.

Stained glass windows with images of haloed saints and the blessed virgin filled the wall. The glass art of Mary holding baby Jesus on a cloud with angels beneath them made me sad. One glance toward the altar with its wooden crucifix told how that story ended.

If Mary couldn't save her son, what hope was there for other sons and their moms?

Hope. That was my problem. I still clung to the little bit of hope I had left.

I looked past Mary and baby Jesus toward the sunlight that poured through them, providing a glimpse outside.

"When we give in to temptation, the enemy wins."

The enemy? My attention returned to Father Truman.

"God uses us in ways that don't always feel positive and we don't always understand."

What the fuck?

"Often it's not *for* us to understand. When people we love, and even those we don't, hurt us, Jesus calls us to love our enemies." Father Truman seemed to be lost in his rhetoric. "But that's not very easy to do, is it?"

Try impossible.

"I know that often the number one emotion ruling my heart, besides my deep, deep love for Gladys Hadley's blueberry buckle," he said with a chuckle, "and Phil Newman's smoked ribs."

The congregation laughed with him and so did I.

"But the emotion that tends to consume me and rule my thoughts is resentment, followed closely by his cousin anger. When I've been hurt by someone, my refusal to forgive that person is often caused by a resentment that's blocking my heart."

This guy's on fire.

I quickly glanced down our pew. My mom looked like she was sleeping with her eyes open. Branson picked at his nails—or what was left of them. Carson was texting. The only family member actually listening to Father Truman's sermon was Jack, who rested his small hand on my knee. For a family that practically took up an entire pew while others stood, only two of us, me and little Jack, were engaged in what was happening.

Sonuva— I stopped myself before finishing the thought and almost laughed. *Isn't that how resentment starts?*

"The hard truth is this: when we lash out at others, regardless of what they did, we injure our souls." Father Truman gripped the side of the podium. "What saves the soul is mercy. God the Father is merciful. Are you? When people have hurt you, are you merciful?"

My thoughts ricocheted in my head like a racquetball

pinging back and forth between my conscious and subconscious with no place to land. Suddenly Jack's hand gripped my knee, which unbeknownst to me had begun to bounce.

"It's okay, Aaron," he whispered.

But my leg was as busy as my mind trying to adjust to Father Truman's sudden off-topic message. Mercy? The guy should've stuck with resentment and anger. Mercy was as misplaced as a nun at a bachelor party. I wasn't sure how I felt about that.

Ambushed. I felt ambushed.

And that pissed me off. It's why I didn't go to mass. I didn't need some pedophile preaching to me about mercy. *Where's God's mercy for my mom? What's up with that shit? Mercy, my ass.*

"The fastest route to mercy is through prayer. Pray for the one who hurts you," Father Truman said.

Praying for someone who hurt me wasn't new, but it wasn't practical.

"When you pray for the person who hurt you, it changes lives," Father Truman continued.

I shook my head. *Nope. It just reminds me how pissed off I actually am.*

"When you can't forgive someone, pray for them. When you pray, the desire for revenge lessens. Nothing good happens when revenge is driving you. This I know."

I was about to grab my jacket and Jack's hand when something in Father Truman's voice made me pause.

"There was someone who had hurt me terribly as a

young man. It was a pain that nearly splintered me off from God. I nursed that grudge the way an alcoholic finds comfort in a bottle. In a perverse way, the more I thought about this individual, the more powerful I thought I became." His gray hair remained stationary while his head swayed from side to side. "But I wasn't powerful. That was the enemy's lie. The enemy fed me that lie, and I ate it up because I didn't want to be the victim. I was willing to do anything so I'd never have to feel victimized again."

My leg stopped bouncing and my thoughts slowed down.

"And in that enemy-fueled thought process, I began to believe that making that individual pay for what they had done to me was just."

It is just.

"Anytime we want someone to pay for what they've done, we lose. Revenge is the fuel that sparks war; it's the rust that erodes families and breaks apart neighborhoods. Revenge is the bitterness that corrodes *your* soul. The only way we win against the enemy of darkness is through prayer. We must always pray for our enemies. Good *can* fight evil through the power of prayer." Father Truman bowed his head before returning to his seat on the dais.

The enemy of darkness.

My leg didn't bounce and my mind settled down as his sermon sank in. I was lost in my thoughts when Jack patted my knee. I glanced at his finger that pointed toward Branson, who was smiling like he had just won the lottery.

"What?" I mouthed silently.

He passed his phone toward me. Snapchat was on the screen. I enlarged the picture of some girl, who looked like she was sitting against a goalpost, with paint on her face and a sign around her neck. She looked bald, or maybe she was an albino. There wasn't much hair there to know.

The Snapchat message posted below the picture read *THOT*, which I knew was slang for "That Ho Over There."

I shrugged and leaned over Jack. "So?" I mouthed back. "Who is she?"

Branson grinned, leaned across Carson, and whispered, "That's the sorority girl from the Albany campus. You know, the one who was so mean." A burst of laughter flew out of Branson, who quickly checked himself before whispering toward me, "That's karma. That's what happens when you make an enemy out of the wrong person."

"Did you do that?" I mouthed when I wasn't sure I wanted to know. During high school, Branson experienced more than one fugue state, which was like a blackout for people with schizoaffective. During those episodes, Trevor commanded Branson's thoughts and actions. At the time, Branson didn't realize that Trevor only existed in his mind. During one, Branson came to in the boys' restroom in our high school with bloody knuckles. Another time he came out of a fugue state on the side of the road in a stolen car with no memory of what led up to either event.

I wouldn't wish a fugue state on anyone. *Nothing good happens.* The only thing they were good for was to realize the person experiencing them was on the cusp of a complete psychotic break from reality.

Branson glanced at his phone and stifled a laugh. "I wish."

When I didn't smile, he shook his head. "No way. It wasn't me, bro. That's messed up," he said a bit too loudly.

Messed up was exactly what Trevor did with Branson's life when he was in command.

Who the fuck knows? Some girl was bound to a goalpost if for no other reason than some sick revenge.

That made me think about Father Truman's message. I leaned against the pew and tried to wrap my brain around his logic. I knew it was his job or vocation or whatever to help save our souls, but something about his message was off.

Harboring resentment or exacting revenge may corrode the soul, but praying for someone in hopes they wouldn't harm me again was like aiming an empty gun at an armed robber. *Pointless.*

Father Truman was right about one thing—someone always got hurt. But it wasn't going to be me.

CHAPTER 15

AARON

I stared at the document on the kitchen table.

<u>LIVING WILL OF TARA LOUISE LAFONTISEE</u>

<u>DIRECTIVE TO PHYSICIANS</u>

<u>DECLARATION</u>

Declaration made this <u>20TH</u> day of <u>OCTOBER</u>. I, Tara Louise Lafontisee, being of sound mind, willfully and voluntarily make known my desire that my dying shall not be artificially prolonged under the circumstances set forth below and do hereby declare:

"What the fuck?" My throat tightened. I glanced toward the front room, but everyone was asleep. Even though it was Monday, no one had school, so no one stirred before nine. It was October, which meant one thing: hunting. Wyoming loved extending weekends because Wyomingites loved hunting.

My flight was scheduled for late afternoon, but I woke early to get a jump on the homework I'd put off so I wouldn't return to Ohio with any regret. Now as I stared at the stack of legal-sized papers on the table beside a note from my mom, regret was all I felt.

Guys, if you have any questions, just ask.
— Mom.

If I have any questions? How 'bout why? Why did you have this drafted?

Instead, I continued reading.

If at any time I should have an incurable injury, disease, or other illness certified to be a terminal condition by two (2) physicians who have personally examined me, one (1) of whom shall be my attending physician, and the physicians have determined that my death will occur whether or not life-sustaining procedures are utilized and where the application of life-sustaining procedures would serve only to artificially prolong the dying process,

I direct that such procedures are to be
withheld or withdrawn, including hydration
and nutrition, and that I be permitted to
die naturally with only the administration of
medication or the performance of any medical
procedure deemed necessary to provide me with
comfort care and to alleviate pain.

Nope. Tears threatened to spill down my face, and I didn't
care. *Why?* She didn't. *She doesn't want life-sustaining
procedures? Who does that?*

She's given up.

I lowered my head, and all the losses and hurt I'd kept so
carefully hidden erupted inside me.

I punched the table with my fist. It stung but not enough.
Then I pounded the table until my knuckles bled and my hand
was numb. But the pain was still there.

"Come on, Mom. I need you to fight."

My cries went unheard. The truth was right in front of me.

2. If in spite of this declaration, I am
comatose, incompetent, or otherwise mentally
or physically incapable of communication, or
otherwise unable to make treatment decisions
for myself, I hereby designate my sister,
Serena Ann Lafontisee, to make treatment
decisions for me, in accordance with my Living
Will Declaration. I have discussed my wishes

concerning terminal care with this person, and I trust her judgment on my behalf.

3.   In the absence of my ability to give directions regarding the use of life-sustaining procedures, it is my intention that this declaration shall be honored by my family and physician(s) and agent as the final expression of my legal right to refuse medical or surgical treatment and accept the consequences from this refusal. I understand the full import of this declaration, and I am emotionally and mentally competent to make this declaration.

4.   If this declaration is to be carried out, I direct that before any life support systems are discontinued, all viable body organs that can be used as transplants in order to prolong the life of another or to replace the body part of another be removed and donated to the appropriate persons or agencies.

5.   This declaration shall be in full effect until it is revoked.

The document was signed and notarized.

No. She wouldn't do that. My mom wouldn't have discussed her wishes concerning terminal care without telling us first. But she had. My aunt knew what she wanted. But in the likely event that my aunt, who lived in Paris, was absent, my mom wanted her family—her children—to honor her intentions against the use of life-sustaining procedures.

But when it came down to it, the child she expected to honor her wishes wasn't Branson, Carson, or Jack. It was me. As the oldest, if even by a minute, my role was solidified. She expected me to tell the doctors to stop trying to save her life.

No. I won't. I will not be the person who pulls the plug on my mother's life. And it pissed me off that she thought I would. Or worse, that I could.

Doesn't she know I would be taking two lives? Hers and mine? Doesn't she care?

I hit my fist against the wall that separated the dining room from her bedroom. I hit the wall again, hoping I'd punch a hole into her room. But I didn't, and there was no response from her. No surprise. My mom had enough painkillers in her bathroom to euthanize a horse. Maybe that was the way to do it. Just check the fuck out. She had, so why not me?

My cell phone buzzed in my jeans pocket. I quickly grabbed it and muted the volume. Jack was still sleeping; no reason to have my little brother wake up to this.

I glanced at my phone. A text from Hannah surfaced on the screen.

Where'd u go?

Home.

When I didn't text back, another message appeared.

Wat happened 2 u?

What didn't happen?

I thumbed the screen to my airline app and searched for an earlier flight. There wasn't anything or anyone here for me, not anymore. I charged my credit card the difference, stuffed my books in my backpack, and texted Hannah.

Ever eat @ an airport?

A laughing emoticon appeared.

Good. Then it's a d8. Meet me @ hopkins international @ noon.

I ripped a sticky note from the counter and intended to let my mom know how fucked up it was to leave what amounted to her goodbye letter on the table. I grabbed a pen and stared at her directive to her physician. The hurt felt wider than the square-shaped paper. Besides, what would I say? *Please don't die? Start fighting? Don't leave me?*

I couldn't swallow. The pain was too great. Maybe this was my penance. I couldn't begin to count all the times I'd let my mom down and disappointed her. Or all the times she had been there for me. The scales weren't nearly balanced.

I wiped my nose on the sleeve of my sweatshirt and wrote what she needed from me. Really the only thing I could give her.

Ma, I'll do it.

I held the pen and stared at the words. *It's not enough.*

She's done everything for me.

I won't let you down. I promise. Love you, Aaron.

I pressed my hands against my eyes to stop the crying, but it didn't work. *Mom. Please.* She filled a space in my heart that was as tender as it got and bruised just as easily. The ache of losing her went directly to that space, and I felt lost. Alone. It was why I'd hopped on a plane and came home. Being home was supposed to fill the void. *When did that stop?*

I gently placed my note on top of her living will, carefully folded the document in thirds, and tucked it inside her purse. There was no need for Branson, Carson, or Jack to find it. Her wishes were mine to bear.

CHAPTER 16

BRANSON

WHEN you wore a badge, no one questioned anything. It was another reason I liked my university parking job— they gave me a badge. And when that shiny piece of silver was attached to the right clothes, like a nice shirt or jacket, it allowed me to roam wherever the fuck I wanted to on campus. And that was exactly what I intended to do.

I wouldn't have to if Professor Nigel wasn't such a douche and accepted late assignments. But he didn't, so here I was in the health sciences building heading toward his biology classroom. It was where the good doctor kept his lecture notes and midterm exam.

Stupid bastard was so old-school he actually still had his tests copied at the college print shop—a little something I discovered when Carmen, who worked part-time at the copy shop, faced a $60 ticket for parking half the day in a two-hour lot. I helped her out of the ticket by not issuing her one, and she spilled the tea on which professors photocopied their exams versus posting them in the university's secure online system.

Sure, it would've been easier for me if Carmen just ran an extra copy of the exam, but I knew she wasn't the type. It was one thing to tell me which professors copied their exams but an entirely different thing to lift it. One amounted to nothing more than gossip while the other could get her expelled from the university.

No biggie. My badge gave me carte blanche to stroll the hallways and enter Nigel's classroom virtually unnoticed, which was exactly what I was going to do.

Classrooms weren't locked until after the last class ended for the night, which gave me about an hour to snap a picture of the midterm on my phone before campus security began their evening patrol. Even then, I doubted they actually checked each doorknob to make sure it was locked. Campus security was lazy. They weren't incentivized—a fancy term for bribe—by a monthly raffle for the parking patrol officer who issued the most tickets. Yeah, I had all the time in the world.

For some reason, plant biology was housed in health sciences. The upside was all the dope student nurses in their tight-fitting scrubs. The downside was the north hallway that was tiled in a black-and-white checkerboard design. I think the tile was supposed to class up the joint and make a statement, but all it did was amp things up. There was enough stress in college without having to face a busy-patterned hallway. Shit, I half expected those creepy twins from *The Shining* to appear at the end of the hall.

I shuddered at the thought. My mind played enough tricks on me; I didn't need any help.

The corridor was clear, but I still glanced in either direction before I entered room 104. A badge could only do so much. I didn't need some male nurse with a fragile ego ratting me out.

With no one in sight, I slipped into his classroom. Nigel's standing desk was tucked in a far corner at the front of the room. The location always seemed off until I realized the distance from the door gave Nigel a clear shot through its windowpane into the hallway. This, of course, gave the sadistic bastard a front row view of the students standing in the hallway because they were locked out. Nigel didn't give two shits if a student was late because of another class running over, or if a student had to hump it across campus because of limited parking, or if their mom announced a second cancer. Late was late, full stop.

If a student was on time for class but their work wasn't, they were still shit out of luck. Nigel wouldn't accept late assignments any more than he'd open the door to late student arrivals. His fucked-up thinking created a real lose-lose dynamic. It wasn't like I didn't know that, of course. It was why when I left Cheyenne to return to Casper, I padded my time knowing I had Professor Douchebag's class.

After a two-hour drive back to Casper, I'd hustled to the health sciences building with ten minutes to spare. But then Hope from Dr. Blaze's office called, and since Nigel wouldn't allow cell phones during class, I stepped out of the room. Only she wasn't calling about a medication refill or to schedule my lab appointment for a blood draw. Nope, Hope called because I'd struck up a conversation with her on Snapchat over the weekend. She called to see what my week looked like and when I'd be back in Cheyenne.

As I watched the minutes tick past too quickly on the clock in the hallway, I made a choice—talk to the redheaded hottie I'd been scoping out for months or be on time for Nigel.

I was sure those in academia would say I made the wrong choice, but I wasn't pursuing a degree in education. *Fuck that*. My degree was in forest management. I had to pass Nigel's class to fulfill a stupid requirement in plant biology. It was lame. One of the most basic forestry rules was clear: if you're not sure, don't eat it. *Duh*. I didn't need some blowhard telling me which plants were dangerous and why. So when Hope called, I followed my heart—something I hadn't done in years.

Following my heart also meant breaking the rules. Since I wasn't on time for his class, I couldn't hand in my assignment. Now, maintaining a passing grade in Nigel's class depended on how well I did on his midterm. And I wasn't about to take any chances.

The room was darker than I'd expected. *Fall forward*. The stupid time change always made it darker earlier. Sure, I liked the longer nights, but when it looked like midnight when it was only six, something wasn't right.

I left the door slightly ajar. I didn't think I could get locked in, but if I didn't have bad luck, I'd have no luck at all.

I activated my cell phone's flashlight and carefully rummaged through Nigel's considerably tall stack of neatly organized, color-coordinated papers. A plants and human health handout was copied on blue paper. I skimmed to the purple section only to find a titillating paper on plant ecology and pathology. *Yawn*. The green pile was, ironically, focused on the topic of green conservation. I moved toward an orange-colored slice of papers when I spotted a hint of pink.

What do we have here?

I glanced at the sheet. "Midterm Exam" was centered across the top, followed by thirty questions that lined the page.

What is double fertilization?

While the first question would normally make me laugh, I knew the answer.

"Double fertilization's a complex but common evolution with flowering plants," I said softly, as if the sound of my own voice would be my downfall.

It was actually one of Nigel's more interesting lectures and slides. I thought about his lecture and the one I'd give.

"I bet you didn't know that after pollination occurs, a second fertilization *can* occur. So in plants, it produces a seeded plant, like corn or peas. But"—I held my finger up as if I were teaching a class in the dark—"when double fertilization occurs in humans, the embryo usually doesn't survive."

I slowly nodded as if empathizing with the empty seats. "I know, sucks."

I leaned my elbow against Nigel's standing desk. "Bet you didn't know I was an identical twin." Again, I nodded toward my imaginary class. I knew time was against me, but in that moment, it felt like the most natural place to be.

"Yup." I surveyed my nonexistent class. "My brother and I started as *one* fertilized egg that split into *two* genetically identical embryos. We share the same face, blood type, and DNA. Although, it makes you wonder how my brother sidestepped the genetic landmine of schizoaffective. Ironically, I have Professor Douchebag to thank for answering that question."

I patted his mile-high stack of papers. "I think the handout was copied on tan? Anyway…."

I thought about the research sheet Nigel gave us. It was somewhere in my apartment. I'd kept it to share with Aaron.

"These scientists in the US, Sweden, and I think the Netherlands?" I shrugged as if accuracy mattered in research. "Anyway, this group of science guys studied something like ten pairs of identical twins, including some where one twin showed signs of dementia or Parkinson's but the other didn't. The takeaway was actually really fascinating and something I wish we had discussed in class." My smile began to fade. "Basically, while my identical twin and I share the same DNA, some of the *coding* in our DNA could be different, which *totally* makes sense."

I stared into the nothingness and realized my fear of public speaking dissipated. I actually spoke better if no one watched me. *I should give* all *my presentations in the dark.*

"You know, it's actually a relief," I said. "My identical

twin and I *aren't* 100 percent similar." I swallowed before concluding my impromptu lecture. "That means my brother, Aaron, will never have to know what it's like to be the divided twin."

The truth was a sobering reality. *The divided twin.*

"And just so you know," I added, trying to lighten the mood for the students I'd never teach, "I'm glad. I wouldn't wish mental illness on anyone—not even Professor Douchebag."

I clapped my hands together. "Anyway, thank you for indulging me." I slightly bowed as if an encore was imminent, then sighed, realizing I'd never be in front of any class. Nope, my classroom was the great outdoors, and that suited me just fine.

I returned my focus to the stack of papers and the next question on the handout, which thankfully was less personal than the first.

What varieties of succulents have water storage leaves?

"I know this. Jade or ice plants." I shrugged. "This *can't* be the midterm." I flicked the cell light toward the header of the paper, but I hadn't misread it. "Midterm Exam" was in bold, front and center.

Damn. This is *it.*

I skimmed the rest of the questions. No surprises.

"Shit. I actually know this."

"That's the intent."

I jumped and dropped my phone. *Fuck!* I quickly

grabbed it and in the process hit the edge of the standing desk. The tower of colorful papers scattered to the floor like confetti. A row of overhead lights flickered, highlighting the ginormous mess. I knelt beside the fragmented rainbow and lowered my head, but the damage was done.

"Mr. Kovak."

I glanced up. He loomed above me with his hands on the hips of his black slacks. His tie swung like a noose around his neck as his dark eyes stared down at me.

"Professor Nigel," I said.

Then he did something I never expected. He extended his hand.

I grabbed it, and he helped me to my feet.

"Would you like to tell me what you're doing in my classroom?"

"Just getting a jump on my attendance." I tried to sell the lie, but Nigel wasn't buying it.

He slowly nodded. "And how would you explain the condition of my classroom?"

"Oh, this?" I surveyed the mess of papers on the floor and scratched the back of my head. "Yeah, *that* was an accident."

I think he may have smiled.

"But nothing that can't be cleaned up," I added, hoping optimism would overshadow the grim reality that my professor just found me with his midterm exam.

I began to gather the papers when he tapped my shoulder.

"Mr. Kovak, that can wait. I think a discussion is in order."

My stomach dropped, and I was pretty sure I broke out in a sweat.

Fuck. I'm a semester away from graduating. What have I done?

Nigel reached the door in three short steps and clicked on the rest of the overhead lights. I held my hand above my eyes while I adjusted to the brightness.

"Please." Nigel nodded toward the table and chairs.

I took a seat behind the first table, and he grabbed a chair and sat opposite me.

"I… I…." I couldn't string together a sentence. Suddenly, I felt myself shatter into a million little pieces. My head pounded with the beat of my heart that was definitely in overdrive. I picked at what nails I had left and tore at my cuticles. Then the coughing kicked in. I knew it was a sign of my tick, but I couldn't help it. It happened when I was nervous or stressed. Or stressed because I was nervous. Every couple of seconds, a little cough escaped without warning.

"I liked your lecture," Nigel said.

And for a minute, I didn't cough, but I kept picking at my nails.

"Have you ever thought about a teaching career?"

My burst of laughter startled us both. A long, drawn-out "No" followed.

He rubbed his chin as if he were assessing the damage in front of him. Or the floor. It was hard to tell which was a bigger mess, me or all the handouts strewn everywhere.

"You mentioned that you're an identical twin," he said.

I nodded.

"Is your brother a student at Wyoming State?"

Again, I laughed. "No, he's serious about education." It came out of my mouth before I could take it back. "I mean, you know, he started here, but then he studied abroad and"—I shrugged—"he found a college that was a better fit."

"I see."

I knew he didn't. No one did. Aaron hadn't fucked up his life like I had. And he sure as shit wouldn't have tried to steal a midterm. Or conduct an impromptu lecture in the process. *What the fuck was I thinking?* I picked at my cuticles until they started to bleed, then placed my hands beneath the table.

"Professor Nigel, I know I shouldn't be here. I was just, you know, worried about the midterm." I sounded pathetic. I cleared my throat and thought about my mom. When any of us got in trouble, she always said half the time she just wanted us to apologize and stop making excuses. "I'm sorry. What I did was wrong."

"Like you said, nothing that can't be cleaned up." He pushed out his chair and turned toward the pile of papers scattered across the floor. "I wouldn't mind a little help," he said with his back to me.

"Right." I hurried toward the clutter and began sorting papers by color, purposefully bypassing the salmon-colored midterm.

I thought he wanted to talk. Was that the talk?

Nigel knelt and his black dress shoes shone against the

tiled floor. *How does anyone get their shoes that shiny?* It should've been the furthest thought from my mind, but I couldn't help but wonder. I could practically see myself in the reflection.

"Mr. Kovak, I'd like you to do something for me."

It felt like the wind was knocked from me. I stopped gathering papers and leaned back on my legs. *Here it comes.*

"Well, actually three things," he said.

I nodded.

"I'd like you to go to the Disability Support Services office." He never broke eye contact with me. "It's in the admin building on the second floor."

Before I could ask why, he continued.

"They provide services for students with disabilities."

"Uh, I don't have a disability."

"I won't insult you by saying that I understand what it's like to live with a mental illness. Or that I knew you had one, because clearly I didn't."

And there it is. I could play the crazy card and ride this thing right out of his classroom. Or....

"Professor Nigel, I'm fine. I take medication and see a shrink. I'm good."

"This is your senior year, isn't it?"

Didn't he hear me? "Uh, yeah."

"Interesting. There's not one notation in your file for accommodations. It's something I would've been notified of at the start of the term. But your name and accommodation aren't noted."

When I didn't respond, he continued. "Accommodations, such as proctored tests, which allow a student to take a test at their own pace, are available for students with a wide range of learning, emotional, or physical disabilities."

"O-kay." I wasn't sure where he was going with this.

"It is quite commendable that you've made it this far in your educational pursuits without testing accommodations in place. Testing situations can be stress producing. Students with hidden disabilities usually drop out," he explained.

Hidden disabilities? Fuck. Just call it what it is—I'm mental. But he kept staring at me, so I shrugged. "It's okay. Really. If anything, I'm sorry you had to hear me ramble. But I'm fine."

"If that were true, I doubt I would've found you in my classroom previewing the midterm exam. Which leads to the second point. I'd like you to write a personal essay about a specific time in your educational experience that shaped you into the young man you are now."

I scoffed. "Okay... may I ask why?"

"Yes, you may. It's the scholarship requirement for graduating seniors who have undergone a unique challenge to finish their education. I think you have a good story to tell. And since I'm the chairperson for the scholarship committee, part of my job is to seek out submissions. So you'd be helping me."

I smiled. "Listen, that's really nice of you, but really, I'm okay. I was in your classroom when I shouldn't have been here."

"You're correct. The Student Code of Conduct is in place

to prevent behavior like this that undermines academic success. However, your lecture is probably what saved you."

I chuckled when I probably should've remained stone-faced.

"So, the first of the two requirements is that you visit the disability offices and write an essay." He paused. "I think your essay will broaden the candidate pool. The deadline for submissions is Friday."

"This Friday?" My voice easily rose an octave.

That time he smiled. "Since you've already got a jump on the study material for the midterm exam, that should give you plenty of time to get an essay typed up. Then in the following week, you can go to the disability office."

I exhaled loud enough for him to hear me. "Sure, okay." I mean, what choice did I have? The guy could've had me suspended from the university, if not worse. "Disability office and essay, got it."

"The final piece is for you to attend at least one group meeting at the Depression Center."

"The Depression Center? Are you for real? I get that depression is one of the symptoms of my illness, but I treat it with medication. And the medication works. I don't get depressed. I mean, I'm starting to *feel* depressed after tonight, but I'm not suicidal or anything." I backed away from Nigel. "Listen, I messed up. Plain and simple. But I can't be the first student who's tried to sneak a glance at a midterm, and I'm pretty sure I won't be the last." As I spoke, I found release in finally sharing my truth and standing up for myself. I wasn't sure what it was, only that there was so much bottled up inside me that I couldn't contain the explosion.

"Actually." I stood and found my footing, both figuratively in the classroom and literally with the rant I felt coming. "I'm kind of shocked that more students aren't here with me. I mean, you *really* leave us no choice. We can't be late, and if we are, you lock us out of the classroom. And then when we're locked out, we can't turn in our assignments. How fucked up is that?"

Nigel remained calm and collected, as if I were reciting the periodic table and not tearing him a new asshole.

"And for the record"—I raised my index finger—"keeping an eye on us in the hallway is just weird. If anyone needs the Depression Center, it's you."

I brushed the sweat from my hands on the side of my jeans, leaving behind two dark prints. "I'd rather take my chances with the dean of students or president or whoever the hell I'm sent to than have to jump through anymore of your hoops. I thought you were actually being cool with all that talk about how great I've done with my mental illness...."

My mental illness was something I shared with strangers at a frat party because they were so drunk I doubted they'd remember. And even if they did, they didn't matter to me. But schizoaffective was a part of myself that I didn't disclose to teachers or anyone who was in a position to use it against me—because over time they would.

"Whatever." I shook my head. "You weren't being cool,

you were just playing another one of your mind games. *Freak.*"

Nigel returned his attention to gathering the papers off the floor as if my outburst was nothing.

I scoffed and turned toward the door. "I don't need this. I don't care what you do to me. I won't let *anyone* mess with my mind again."

He cupped his knees and stood. It was something my old man did. And I always popped up from a kneeling position whenever he did it, like a reminder that youth was on my side. I would've done the same thing to Nigel, but I was already standing.

I grabbed the handle and the door swung open more quickly than I anticipated, almost knocking me in the face.

"Mr. Kovak."

"What?" My tone was terse.

"I lock the door after class begins as a safeguard. Campus security and student safety—*your* safety—is a top priority for me." He leaned against the front table and went quiet for a minute. When he spoke again, his voice was different, softer. "I was teaching *right* here in this classroom." He tapped his finger on the table. "I was right here when it happened."

"What happened?" I still didn't care how my tone came off, though it seemed to have lost a slight bit of the edge it had before.

"My dear, dear friend and colleague Dr. Kincaid was killed by his daughter." Nigel started twisting the ring on his finger. It looked painful, but I understood. Sometimes physical pain was easier to deal with.

"Dr. Kincaid and I went to grad school together."

I remembered the story. I was in the mental ward of the hospital when it happened, but the headline was unforgettable. "Daughter Kills Father" was plastered on every newspaper and shown on every cable channel. It was like some Greek tragedy, only it really happened—and in Casper, Wyoming, no less.

"It was fall, so when Dottie—that was his daughter— showed up on campus with a compound bow, no one thought otherwise."

Hunting. It was the one part of the forest service I hated, enforcing hunting regulations. It'd just be easier if hunting was eliminated. Hell, if wild animals like the gray wolf and grizzly bear were as fiercely protected as Wyoming's right to bear arms, they wouldn't be endangered and a father would still be alive. But this was Wyoming. Owning a gun, weapon, or compound bow was tantamount to manhood. Or in this case womanhood.

"I didn't see it happen, but students told me," he said. "Dottie walked into the classroom, drew back the bowstring, and fired an arrow." The memory of the event was etched on his face. "And then she shot another arrow, and another."

"I can't imagine," I said truthfully.

"It was pure chaos. Students ran past my classroom screaming and crying. I didn't know what happened. I thought maybe someone got sick. You know, sometimes the nursing students get sick during dissection labs." He looked at me, a plea for understanding filling his eyes. "I didn't know. How could I?"

He stared at me, waiting for an answer, but there wasn't one.

"Jesus" was all I said.

"I managed to stop a student, and that's when I heard." He cupped the back of his neck as if cradling the grim memory. "I ran to Bryan's classroom, but she had locked the door. She locked herself inside with him, with her father. He couldn't get out, and no one could get in."

"Damn."

"By the time the police arrived, well"—his voice dropped—"it was too late. They were both dead."

Nigel dropped his hand and slightly tilted his head. "There was speculation that Dottie suffered from Asperger's, but that's all it was, speculation. I do know that she suffered horribly from depression. Bryan often spoke about the treatment centers she went to for her depression."

Oh, I get it. "Is that why you want me to go to the Depression Center, because you're afraid I'm gonna go all postal on you?"

He waved his hands like he was trying to flag down a moving train. I was sure with the way I'd run him over with my rant, that was how it felt.

"No, not at all. But I hope it explains why I lock my classroom," he said. "After Bryan's death, we had mandatory training on school shootings and shooters. The proposed logic is that a locked door is a deterrent to an active shooter."

"Or you're locking yourself in with the danger," I said.

"Exactly my thinking!" His eyes flashed with life. "I couldn't agree more. By their logic, we're locking out danger, but we could very well be locking ourselves in with danger as well." He rolled his eyes. "But I'm just a cog in the wheel."

I laughed. "Seriously? You have tenure, which makes you untouchable." My mom had worked in higher education my entire life. She had her own rants about education, but tenure wasn't one of them. Tenure was as good as it got.

"I knew your mother," he said. "I didn't... uh... well, I wasn't a very supportive colleague."

I shrugged. "She lost her career because of me."

The lines around his eyes wrinkled even more.

"When I was in my illness." I stopped. "No, I mean before I got the help I needed, my mom read my English journal, which basically made her mad at this girl because she thought she was bullying me. It's a long story, but"—I scratched my head—"she tried to protect me and lost her job in the process."

"I'm sorry. That must've been difficult," he said.

"It's not something I'm proud of, but we've all moved on from it."

"That's good to hear. Please tell her I said hello."

I swayed my head slowly from side to side. "Man, I don't get you. If you knew my mom, why now? Why tell me this? Why make a connection now?"

"Fair questions," he said. "But to back up a moment, I told you about the tragedy on campus because I thought it was important that you understood my reasoning behind the locked door. And I suppose I did want to make a connection with you."

"Okay. I get locking the door and not keeping it open because that's how that girl got in and did what she did. But if a student's late, why can't you open the door? I mean, if they're armed with some weapon, don't you think you'd see it?"

He grinned. "Valid point. I could be a bit more...." He paused. He did the same thing during his lectures, like he was searching for just the right word. "Flexible," he said finally. "I could be a bit more flexible."

I crossed my arms. "So why the Depression Center? I mean, I get the essay and the disability office, but...."

"The Depression Center helped me after Bryan's shooting," he admitted. "I suffered, and I supposed I still suffer at times, from PTSD."

I thought about Blaze and how he'd said PTSD was caused by anxiety—extreme anxiety. "I mean, I get that what I did was wrong by coming into your classroom, but the Depression Center? That just seems *way* extreme. I was just trying to get a look at the midterm. I wasn't hacking into your computer to change my grade or destroy your classroom." I held up my hand in my defense. "Granted, that *still* happened, but it was never my intent."

I'd never heard Professor Nigel laugh. It was almost like a wheeze, but even better than that, his entire face looked ten years younger.

"Mr. Kovak, you have a wonderful sense of humor.

Well timed."

"So does that mean the Depression Center is off the table?"

Again, he wheezed a laugh. "Yes, yes. Though I'd still like you to write an essay for the scholarship." He raised a finger. "I can't force you to go to the Depression Center or go to the disability office. However, I think both would benefit you greatly."

"Yeah, I can check into the disability office." I paused a moment, contemplating. "But I'm not making any promises about the Depression Center. Thanks, you know, for not…." I wasn't sure what to say.

"Well, even Professor Douchebag has his days," he said, which made me laugh.

"Oh, damn. You heard that?"

He slowly nodded. "Like I said, you gave quite a stirring lecture."

"I was…." I rolled my eyes. "Well, I don't know *what* I was doing." I glanced toward the hallway and its busy design. I imagined blood splattered across the black-and-white tiles. It was just where my mind traveled. "So, essay by Friday and disability services the following week?"

When Nigel smiled, it had the same effect as his laughter. He looked like an entirely different guy. "That would be fine."

"Okay, so do I just email *you* the essay?"

"Yes. I'll make sure it gets into the right hands."

"Cool."

"Have a good night, Mr. Kovak."

"Yeah, you too."

That time when I walked into the hallway, I no longer worried about what or who was hiding around the corners.

CHAPTER 17

AARON

TWENTY minutes remained in Professor Whitman's class. Even though her PowerPoints were usually top-notch, today's topic on the foundation of democracy and how it'd been implemented in different countries wasn't only a yawnfest, it was pointless.

Sure, there were different types of democracy, but at the end of the day, it didn't matter. If a country had a parliament, congress, president, or prime minister but practiced democracy, then they represented the will of the people. Regardless of the system or how fancy it was named, the bottom line was the same: the decision-making processes were for the people, which made the entire conversation useless and boring. *So boring.*

But since attendance was mandatory and I had already blown through my three allotted absences, I was stuck.

However, on a high note, Professor Whitman was in a blinding yellow outfit. I couldn't look away from the podium if I wanted to. The glare from her clothes was like a gravitational pull, but it was the first time she'd worn something other than black. With her Harry Potter-like glasses and standard black suits covered by a long black jacket, she looked suited to teach at Hogwarts. But today in her yellow top with matching jacket and pants, she reminded me of the Man with the Yellow Hat in Jack's *Curious George* books. All she was missing was the hat.

When Jack was much younger, I used to read to him. His favorite book was a collection of George's misadventures. Jack loved that curious little character so much that when I took him shopping for a Mother's Day gift and we passed a shelf of stuffed monkeys, I pointed to one.

"Jack, what's this?"

"It's a George," he'd said.

The more I stared at Professor Whitman, the more I thought of home.

It made no sense. A week ago, I was home and couldn't wait to leave. Now I wanted to return.

I pulled out my phone and started going through people's stories on Snapchat.

A picture of Caleb and Big Mike surfaced. They were guys I'd met when we all studied abroad. Instead of staying in Jordon on the weekends, we headed to the airport and traveled wherever Ryanair flew. The tickets were unbelievably cheap, and as long as we packed our shit in a backpack, it didn't cost anything extra. In Morocco we visited the Blue City, in Rome we toured the Colosseum, and in the Sahara we rode camels. I couldn't have asked for better travel partners. We visited the most beautiful places and drank the best ales, wines, and whatever the locals handed us. It was awesome.

The picture of my boys at their homecoming football game at Columbus University made me thumb over to my message app. The last text from Hannah appeared.

Hey, I'm heading to my parents' house 4 w/end. Last chance to join me!

A smile returned to my face. *Sweet Hannah*. I wasn't ready to meet the parents, so I passed. I didn't even make up an excuse, just texted **Next time**.

But now I had no weekend plans. I tapped my thumbs against the side of my phone. Columbus was an easy two-hour drive away. Not that I had a car, but there was always Greyhound.

That was what I needed—an adventure. Halloween was coming up, and I'd bet CU would be a fuckfest. Girls dressing slutty and guys showing off their masculinity.

I group-texted Caleb and Mike.

Yo itz bn a while. We should chill agn.

It didn't take long for Caleb to reply.

Hell yeah. Hallo- w/end. We're goin as a tequila shot: salt, lime, n tequila. We're lookin 4 our 3rd amigo! When u comin?

My fingers couldn't text fast enough.

Checkin Greyhound now. Packin a bag & I'm outta here.

With a plan in place for the weekend, my loneliness vanished just as quickly as Professor Whitman's class ended.

I'd just started for the door when my name was called.

"Mr. Kovak, a moment."

I cocked my head toward the podium at the bottom of the lecture hall. Professor Whitman's cupped hand beckoned me forward. My classmates brushed past me like a herd of wild animals suddenly set free. *Lucky bastards.*

"Professor Whitman," I said when I approached.

The lenses in her black-framed glasses were thick and made her eyes practically bug out of her face.

"Mr. Kovak, you haven't given me or your classmates your hundred percent." She paused, and I said nothing. What was there to say? She was right.

"If you want to pass this class, you need to give the class discussions more than you're giving," she continued.

"Understood. I'll participate more," I said.

"Was there something about the topic that disinterested you?"

Where to begin?

"No, not at all." But I could tell from the pained expression and her squinty eyes that she expected more. She needed something to assure her that it wasn't her lecture or the topic of democracy that nearly put me to sleep.

"My mom's cancer spread from her breasts to her ovaries," I blurted out like I was back in elementary school and not a senior in college.

But it did what I'd hoped. Her expression changed, turning from irritation to sympathy.

"I'm sorry to hear that," she said. "We have trained counselors on campus who can help during this transition."

Counseling? No thanks. Been there, got the T-shirt. But I said what was expected of me. "Thanks, I'll look into that."

"If you need an extension on the paper that's due Monday," she started, but my face must have conveyed my surprise that a paper was even due, because she continued, "I believe you chose the topic of refugees?"

"Right." At one time, refugees were *the* most saturated topic in the news. But that was months ago. *Fuck.*

"Have it to my office by Wednesday of next week," she offered.

"Will do. Thank you."

My phone buzzed in my back jeans pocket, and I knew it was Caleb or Big Mike wondering when I'd be in Columbus.

I nodded toward my professor. "I'll make more of an effort in class."

"That's all I ask." Her nod was my cue to exit.

I was careful not to take the lecture hall stairs two at a time, lest I look too anxious. But once I was outside the building, I glanced at the text from Mike.

Pick u ^ @ station.

And just like that, my weekend plans took shape.

Talk about the freaks on the bus. For more than two hours, I listened to a man talk to himself and considered introducing him to my brother. Of course, I wouldn't, but the thought kept me entertained and took my mind off the floor that my shoes stuck to. *Nasty.*

As if my first ride on a Greyhound wasn't enough of

a shit show, as soon as I stepped off the bus and walked outside the station, a homeless guy immediately approached me.

"Where you from?" he said, crowding me.

"Toledo."

"Oh, you're a LeBron fan?"

"Yeah, I guess." I made my way toward the sidewalk, where two more homeless dudes descended upon me.

"This one's a LeBron fan," the first homeless guy said.

"Oh, you know he's a Trump supporter and a racist," another chimed in.

Three black men surrounded me. And they all began talking.

"Hey, whatever you need, we can get it for you," one guy said.

"Nah, he's a Trump fan. He don't need nothing," another replied.

With so many different voices going on all at once, it was like having schizophrenia. I choked down my laughter. It was just what I did in stressful situations, make stupid, inappropriate jokes.

"You a Trump supporter, aren't you?" the first man asked again.

"Whatever, man, I've gotta go." I tried to push past the circle I felt enclosed in.

"Make America Great Again," the guy called out.

I finally raised my voice, which seemed to get their attention. "Guys, I don't have time for this."

I broke free and stood on the curb, hoping like hell Caleb

and Mike wouldn't keep me waiting.

Within minutes, a black Subaru pulled alongside me.

"You getting heckled by the homeless?" Caleb asked, and I laughed.

I threw my bag in the back seat and slid in behind Big Mike. He was called that not because he was fat but because he was fucking muscular as hell. When he turned around in the passenger seat, the weight in the car shifted. *The guy's a beast.*

"Bet you don't have a lot of homeless in Toledo," he said.

"I dunno. I don't leave campus much. But for real, like my biggest fear is being in a poor part of town, surrounded by black people, in a city I don't know." I paused, thinking it over. "So, yeah, my biggest fear just realized."

"Black people? What the fuck, Aaron?" Caleb said.

"Listen, guys, I grew up in Wyoming where there's no diversity. I never saw a black person, didn't really know about LGBTQ, nor did I ever hear varying opinions or ideologies on anything. I grew up in a small town surrounded by small white people. I'm afraid of cities, public transportation, and homeless people," I explained. "It's like I'm afraid of diversity because I was raised in such a red, racist state." Again I paused and thought about what I was saying. "Okay, maybe I'm not a racist in the traditional sense. I'm more like an accidental racist."

They both laughed.

"I'll tell you this, though," I said, "I won't raise *my* kids in Wyoming."

"Why? I thought Wyoming was great," Mike said.

"Sure, if you want to raise a conservative racist who's afraid of cities and people of color, then Wyoming's your place."

"Ah, shit, every place has issues," Caleb cut in.

"True." I leaned forward. "But there's nothing for me in Wyoming anymore."

"What about your twin brother?" Mike asked. "Branson, right?"

"Yeah, good memory. Bran's going into forestry with the national parks. He can work anywhere. We both want to put Wyoming in our rearview and never look back."

"Understood, man, understood," Caleb said.

Mike turned toward Caleb and then me. "It smells like weed."

I laugh. "Yeah, that's me." I fanned the collar of my shirt, but if anything it just wafted the skunky smell of weed around the car.

"You smoking? No way." Caleb stared at me in the rearview mirror. "In Jordon you were the purest. You wouldn't smoke pot, hashish, or do anything. All you did was drink."

"Yeah, and you and Mike ruined me," I said. "Plus, you told me enough times that I was the nicest guy in the world. Like the nicest guy you'd both ever met. I don't know if I believe that, but it's what you said."

"So what does that have to do with smoking weed?" Caleb asked.

"After hearing that shit for an entire semester, I felt like some pussy. When I transferred from Wyoming to Ohio, I decided it needed to be more than a geographical change. It needed to be a state of mind." I raised my fingers in the peace sign like a stoner on a good trip.

Again they laughed.

"But really? Pot? Is that your *new* state of mind?" Caleb asked.

"Shit. Like you don't smoke," I countered.

"I cut down."

I scoffed, and Mike turned around to look at me. "No, really, he has. The pot was really messing with his thinking."

I rolled my eyes. "Okay."

"Legit. The last time I got really stoned, I thought Mike was trying to steal something from me and I went after him," Caleb said. "It was intense. It was like I became someone else."

"Well, I don't know what the fuck *you're* smoking, but pot hasn't done anything like that to me, so stop killing *my* buzz," I told him. "Besides, getting high was the only way I made it through that fucked-up bus ride."

When neither of them said anything, I hit the back of Mike's seat. "So, Hallo-weekend, brother!"

"Get ready for crazy," Mike said.

"Already there."

The music from the house party was nightclub loud. It was also so dark that I kept bumping into people.

"You get used to it," Caleb said.

Our white T-shirts practically glowed in the living room. The neon green stenciling didn't hurt either. Since my chest announced that I was Lime, I stood beside Caleb, who was Tequila, and Big Mike, who was Salt. Together we were a tequila shot.

Big Mike looked dope with a shirt that barely fit him. *What a monster.* But Caleb was a goddamn stud with *GQ*-like modeling skills that he used when the hostess of the house party snapped our picture with an instant camera.

"Tequila shots never looked so good," she said with a saucy wink while she fanned the pic.

"Shake it like a Polaroid," Mike said, which was lame as hell but seemed to work on the hostess, who was dressed like a Starbucks coffee. She even had a hat with a green straw, which was pretty damn funny.

Everyone at the party looked like they belonged in an Abercrombie & Fitch commercial. They were ridiculously hot, and the party atmosphere had this intense, high-energy that kept everyone in a heightened state. Or maybe it was the drugs. There was enough weed, Oxy, and Adderall to fill the football stadium.

We quenched anyone and everyone's thirst with shots. I squeezed lime into any open mouth that approached me, Caleb filled the shot glass, which he handed out like candy, and Big Mike poured salt on his arm that girls lined up to lick. Together we were unstoppable. For every shot Mike poured for a girl, he poured one for me.

Before I knew it, I was drunk off my ass. When we discovered there was a pony keg upstairs, Caleb and I headed to the second-floor balcony. I started tapping it and it sounded full, but I had to be sure, so I lifted it.

"Fuck." I set it down. "That's got like three-fourths left. It's still heavy."

"Cool" was all Caleb said.

"Listen, man, I'm going to steal it," I told him.

"What?"

"I'm going to put the keg on the railing and pretend like it fell over while I was getting a drink."

The plan made perfect sense both in my head and when I shared it with Caleb, who nodded like I had just hatched the best idea ever. I checked to make sure I wouldn't hit anyone, then hefted the keg to the edge of the white railing, but instead of acting like I was pumping the keg like I'd planned, I just pushed it over the side. It fell hard and loud.

Caleb and I burst out laughing. We peered over the ledge and saw the pony keg upside down on the lawn.

"Dude!" Caleb slapped me on the back. I didn't think he was as drunk or as stoned as me. "What the fuck?"

I gripped his shoulder. "Come on! It's ours for the taking!"

I ran down the stairs with Caleb on my heels, racing out the front door and toward the keg that had rolled on its side. I hefted it up, tucked it against me like a football, and started running. It may have only been a pony keg, but it was almost full and I ran like the wind—easily and effortlessly. *Yeah, who's got buggy whip arms now? Take that, sorority bitch!*

All I heard behind me was the sweet sound of Caleb and Big Mike's laughter. I didn't stop running until I reached

Caleb's apartment. I set the keg beside his front door and grabbed the tap. My desire for something cold outrode reason. I didn't have a cup, but that didn't matter. I'd guzzle straight from the hose.

Only the keg wouldn't pump. I leaned forward and realized that when it landed, it smashed the tap.

"Fuck." I ran my sweaty hands through my hair.

Caleb reached me first. "Dude, you're a wild man."

I shrugged. "Yeah, well, the fucking pump's broken."

Mike arrived just in time to hear my pathetic declaration and burst out laughing. "Still, best beer heist ever."

But instead of feeling happy, shame crept over me like a heavy cloak that weighed me down. *I fucked up.* First I got called out after class for not participating and now this? I shouldn't have stolen the keg. I didn't know if it was Father Truman's sermon or Professor Whitman or what, but I couldn't shake how awful I felt in that moment.

I'm letting everyone down.

"We should return it," I told them.

"Uh, no," Caleb said.

"Yeah, that's *not* a good idea," Mike echoed.

Was it? Was anything I'd done from the moment I left campus a good idea?

I could be with Hannah right now. Why didn't I go with her? What's my fucking problem?

I glanced at the keg and contemplated my options.

"Why buy trouble that isn't there?" Caleb said.

"What the fuck does that mean?" I stared at my friend, who I thought I knew, but now I wasn't so sure.

"Aaron, folks here aren't as cool as they are in Toledo," Mike said.

"Dude, you got away with it. Now let's go inside my apartment and try to crack this thing open," Caleb said by way of an explanation, but something still felt off.

Fucking everything was off.

I came to Columbus so I wouldn't feel alone, but this wasn't my school or campus. With Caleb and Mike both staring at me, I suddenly felt like a third wheel.

"Listen, they've got two other kegs on the balcony. They aren't going to miss one," Mike said.

They both made valid points, but this wasn't a democracy. The choice was mine and mine alone to make. *I've got to do something.*

"You don't have to come with me, but I've got to take it back." Anxiety inched up my chest, making it hard to breathe.

"Hey, buddy, it's okay. Everyone steals things at parties," Mike said. "One time I took this really dope bottle opener." He glanced at Caleb. "Remember that?"

"For real." Caleb gripped my shoulder. "Dude, it's no big deal. You're tripping. Besides, the keg's broken."

The dented keg and busted pump made my stomach tighten. "Man, I blew it." I rubbed my hands on my jeans. "I've got to make this right."

CHAPTER 18

AARON

HER name was Amber, and originally I thought she was dressed as a Starbucks coffee.

"I'm a Frappuccino," she corrected me with a curtsy that was cute as hell.

"What flavor?" I raised a single eyebrow. It always worked well with the finer sex.

"I don't know!" She laughed and then raised her own eyebrow. "What's your favorite?"

"Strawberries and cream." I felt heat rush to my face. Thankfully, she laughed. I nodded toward the top of her head. "Is that PVC pipe?"

"Yes! How'd you know?"

"My dad works with it at the golf course. They use it for the irrigation system." My summers spent in Jackson Hole flashed before me. After so many countless hours literally laying pipe, I could practically feel the smooth material that protruded from her head in a makeshift straw. "I didn't know they made it in green."

She slightly bowed and her long, wavy brown hair brushed against her bare, tanned shoulder. She was showing off the green PVC pipe that was stuck in a bubble of white felt, which actually did look like whipped cream, but I couldn't stop staring at her hair. Or the way it fell so far down her arm.

"Nice," I said.

Brown eyes gazed up at me. A guy could lose himself in those eyes. She had perfect teeth and a perfect smile. Everything about her was perfect—except she wasn't Hannah.

I grabbed the bottle of bourbon on the kitchen counter, twisted off the cap, and began to drink. The sooner I forgot about Hannah, the better my night would go.

"Sorry about your keg," I said.

She grinned. "It's not really *my* keg, but the deposit on it is. Thanks for finding it."

I shrugged. There was only so much truth-telling I was willing to do. "Eh, it was the right thing to do."

"Are you always such a Boy Scout?" She bridged the gap between us, which in the crowded kitchen wasn't much.

I shook my head. "Rarely."

Whenever she smiled, her head tilted. "I'm not a fan of good."

"No?" I held her gaze with my own.

"No." Her hair swayed on her shoulders. "Why be good when bad is so much more fun?" The rest of her costume consisted of nothing more than a tan-colored slip that made her look like she wasn't wearing anything. The oversized green Starbucks logo in the center of her stomach—not that she had a belly—distinguished her outfit as a costume and not just some sexy lingerie. The girl was tiny with a big personality that I couldn't drink in enough.

I took another hard swig from the bottle. The rush of bourbon heated my throat and loosened the imaginary hand that always seemed wrapped around my neck, waiting to choke the life out of me.

"So...." I crossed the last bit of space between us until our bodies touched. Even though the house screamed with people, everything and everyone faded to black. Her brown eyes and bewitching smile were all I saw.

She stood on her tiptoes until her lips pressed against mine. There were two guarantees when I was drunk: I was a shitty driver, and I was horny as hell. Since I didn't have a car, there was no worry about the former, and the latter seemed to be working itself out quite nicely. When her tongue slipped into my mouth, the tang of lemonade awakened my senses. When she led me toward her upstairs bedroom, nothing else mattered for a moment and I was happy.

CHAPTER 19

BRANSON

I scanned the waiting room. One guy's leg was bouncing and a gal was knitting either a giant sock or sweater, but it was the dude in the heavy tweed winter coat with the yellow flower in his lapel that truly shined. The room was hot as fuck, and this cat looked like he was ready for Wyoming's worst winter. I watched him look frantically around the place. *Yeah, buddy, no one's in charge.*

"I'm dyslexic," he announced. "Can anyone help me fill out this form?"

I addressed him from the aluminum chair that my huge ass was parked on.

"Buddy, I've got good news and bad news. The good news is that I'm not dyslexic, but the bad news is that in stressful situations, I tend to hear voices. So if you speak up, then I can do it. I can help ya."

"Voices, huh?"

No one in the room stared at me or thought twice about

my revelation or our conversation. Shit, I was in a room full of people who were probably more like me than I wanted to own. Add to it that we were all here on our weekend, which either made us total losers or desperate to get a professor off our backs. Or probably both.

"Yeah, that's a whole other story." I stood and walked toward him. "Let's get the form filled out together."

"Thanks, man," he said and handed me the clipboard.

"Welcome to the Depression Center," I read from the pink intake sheet I'd completed ten minutes earlier.

The guy grinned. "Why would they welcome you to a center for depression? Isn't that counterproductive?"

I laughed. "Good point. Maybe it's about relating."

That made him chuckle.

"I'm more likely to get overwhelmed with all this stuff," he said.

"Me too."

I discovered his name was Bob Carole. He was two years older than me and about to graduate.

"I didn't think I'd ever get a college degree. So to be under thirty is a win," he said.

"Dude, you're only twenty-five. You know how many people take gap years? You're right on course."

Bob seemed to consider what I said.

"My professor told me this was the best opportunity for me to meet *my* people," he told me.

If I had a dime for every time well-intentioned people and their well-intentioned comments told me what I needed, I'd be as rich as Trump and just as emotionally bankrupt.

"Hell, Bob," I said, "I think I just found my tribe."

My first session with the Depression Center began when the counselor ushered us into a sterile room with white walls and more aluminum chairs. She introduced herself as Gabbie but pronounced her name through gritted teeth so it sounded more like Debbie. Still, she was in charge and asked us to grab a chair and form one large circle.

If it wasn't such a stereotype of group therapy, I'd laugh. But I'd already made a friend in Bob, who kicked off the conversation. Gabbie wanted us to introduce ourselves and the *issue*—singular—we were working on.

"So, my mom claims there was a time when there weren't laptops. Strange," Bob began. His coat was unbuttoned, which revealed another jacket on top of a sweatshirt and sweatpants. The guy was either seriously cold or trying to cut weight for wrestling. And with the gut that hung over his pants, I doubted he was a wrestler.

"Then IBM invented the first portable computer, and the thing was huge. Like not just in the newness of it but also the actual size. This thing came with a carrying case and had like zero battery life. Still, as my mom tells the story, it was transformative, or so she claims," he continued.

I glanced at Gabbie, who sat with her legs shifted to the side and crossed at the ankle like she was royalty. Or maybe that was how women sat. It just looked weird. And uncomfortable as fuck.

"Anyway, since my mom had one of the first laptops, she

said it made her feel less invisible, which is funny because all my life, I've wanted to be invisible and she didn't." Bob seemed lost in time.

Still, Gabbie said nothing, which prompted Bob to continue.

"So as computers advanced, my mom continued to invest in them, which was like a second mortgage," he said. "But when I was little and couldn't read or write like my brothers and sister, she put me on the computer. I still struggled to read, and my numbers always got mixed up, but it's like my brain was hardwired for computers. The keyboard and everything. It all just made sense to me. Funny, right?" Bob made eye contact with me, and I nodded. "Everyone liked to tell my mom that her approach to my dyslexia was crazy, but sometimes it's that crazy that makes all the difference."

Fuck yeah, Bob. Immediately I thought of my mom. When I told her about the static, which was what I called the voices in my head, she did everything to make it go away. My mom's belief in me was so steadfast that she was completely blindsided when she realized that my command hallucination, Trevor, had been calling the shots. Still, it didn't stop her. If anything, it made her work harder to get me the help I needed—at any cost. What she did to save me wasn't crazy to me, but I knew my dad questioned her sanity.

"It's well-meaning parents and caregivers who often integrate and normalize our mental health challenges. Instead of having this difference," Gabbie said, "it sounds like your mom normalized it."

"Straight up. I'm not thrilled about being here, but if it helps me go from failing a class to graduating, I'll do it," Bob replied.

"What class?" The girl with the knitting needles stopped long enough to make eye contact.

"Algebra. I've taken the class three times," Bob said.

"I'm going to graduate on time and in the top of my class," the knitter stated, which gave me another reason to dislike her.

"Everyone's course is their own," Gabbie said. "Bob, do you have your accommodations in place?"

"Yeah, I use the testing lab. I take all my tests there without any disruptions, but sometimes I need absolute quiet, and that doesn't always happen."

Gabbie reached beside her chair for a yellow pad of paper and ballpoint pen and wrote something down. "There's other accommodations for proctored tests where it's just you and the proctor alone in a room."

"Cool," Bob said.

"Who's next?" Gabbie barely glanced around the circle before she nodded from Bob to me.

"I'm Branson. I have schizoaffective disorder, and sometimes it's hard to drown out the sound when I'm writing papers or taking a test."

"Okay." Her face neither scrunched up nor did she take a measured step back with her chair. The look on her face actually seemed genuine. "Have you thought about using the language lab?"

I shook my head.

"It's a free service on campus that helps students with editing and proofing," she explained.

"And I'm sure they don't battle with multiple voices competing with each other for top spot." I relied on humor to deflect real emotion. I half laughed, but she didn't. Instead, her face softened.

"You have a condition, but...."

But. That three-letter word negated everything that went before it. I glanced away. I knew the drill. Blah, blah, blah, *but* it's your responsibility to take care of your illness. *But* you can't expect everyone to understand. *But* you're the one who entered your professor's office and tried to steal the midterm. *But* this falls on you.

"Branson?"

I resumed eye contact.

"What do you wish people knew about you?" she asked.

"What?"

I wasn't sure I heard her correctly. No one had ever asked me that question.

"What do you wish people knew about you?"

"That I'm not a label. I'm *not* my mental illness. It's not like I go around telling people I have schizoaffective, but when people find out?" I shrugged. "I want to say, 'Check your assumptions.' Not everyone with a mental illness like schizoaffective, bipolar, or whatever it is is going to go shoot up a movie theater or school campus."

Gabbie gently smiled, but it was Bob who spoke.

"Yeah, like don't get caught in the stigma that's attached to mental illness," he said. "We all have *issues*, but who doesn't?"

He elbowed me. "'Check your assumptions' is legit. Maybe we should get that made into a sticker. Like with a big check mark. I'd do it, but then it might read 'assumptions' with a big check." Bob elbowed me again. "Actually, that could work too."

His logic made perfect sense.

"Stickers really *only* work if there's a defined purpose," knitting girl said.

If I weren't on a regular dose of medicine, which kept the shadow people that committed heinous acts in my mind at bay, my divided mind would've had a field day with her. I knew the shadow people well enough to know they'd use her fucking knitting needles to shut her down permanently. But I was on meds, so the thought passed as soon as it entered.

As it was, the knitter went next. "I'm Barbara and I have an anxiety disorder," she said. "It's why I took up knitting. If I can focus on one thing, then I won't worry about all the other stuff. Plus, it helps me concentrate." She resumed knitting. Black and gray yarn wove through her fingers like she was spinning an intricate web. "I'm socially awkward, and I have a fear of heights." She paused to make eye contact with Gabbie. "The heights thing isn't related to my anxiety. It's just a thing. I probably shouldn't have it, but I do."

"Self-deprecating helps no one. Let's not *should* on ourselves," Gabbie said to the group. "A fear of heights is a fear of heights." She laughed. "I'm not a fan of bridges. Like Bob said, we all have our stuff. And to circle back to the issue Branson raised about assumptions, it's natural to want to correct misgivings people have about your mental health. And in the right context, a meaningful conversation can occur. Often, though"—she glanced my way—"when these comments are made, we may not be in the best headspace to have that meaningful conversation. Sometimes it's healthier to walk away from the conversation and return to it later."

"Yeah, I don't agree with that," Bob said. "It's like you're giving a pass to all the assholes out there who bully and shame us."

She slowly shook her head, and her short black hair barely swayed. "What I'm suggesting is to pause. Pause when agitated or confronted and allow yourself the opportunity to reflect on what's happening. All too often we react, which in the offender's mind is all they need to feed their misconception about mental health. When we react, we lose the opportunity to respond."

My thoughts turned to Hope. During our first date, she was so surprised that I listened before I responded. I guess she was so used to people interrupting her at work and making assumptions about her because she worked for a shrink that when I listened, I mean *really* listened to her, she about cried. We'd been texting ever since. When she told me she didn't like to be alone, with the exception of this weekend, we spent all our days off together.

Gabbie moved her crossed legs and shifted gears. "We're here to support each other. You may not understand what someone is working through or their process, which is why offering support is the great equalizer."

"Hundred percent," Bob said. "Branson helped me with

my paperwork, and the dude didn't even blink when I said I was dyslexic. Do you know how many people turn away from me when I ask for help? It's like they're afraid that dyslexia is contagious or something." He leaned forward in his chair. "It's not contagious."

"All valid points," Gabbie said, then prompted the next student to share.

When Bob sat back in his seat, he turned to me. "We should totally hang out."

I was in a room full of rejects, not where I expected to spend part of my weekend. Yet other than issuing parking tickets, this was the most fun I'd had on campus in a long, long time. I knew I had Professor Nigel to thank, but something about the way he'd practically blackmailed me into this self-help group still pissed me off. He was just another link in a chain of well-meaning people who thought they could fix me.

I didn't need fixing. But I did need a friend.

"Text yourself my number." I handed my cell phone to Bob, which I realized was probably backward from how it should be done, but my logic made perfect sense to him.

CHAPTER 20

DAVID AND ME

"BONITA! I'm back." I'd barely set foot in my apartment when a rancid odor overwhelmed me. The trash can was upturned, and garbage sprawled across the kitchen.

"You fat whore. You went through so much shit." Something black and nasty was stuck to the linoleum.

"What is this?" I flipped on the overhead light and crouched beside the oven. The plastic bag that once held a dozen cinnamon-raisin bagels was torn to shit, and the remnants of a raisin were practically cemented to the floor. A soft meow, like an apology, began from the living room and continued until my Siamese cat appeared beside me in the kitchen.

"Look what you did." I pointed to the mess. "I wasn't even gone that long. Are you happy?" Her tail gently brushed against my leg. "You better not be."

She jumped to the counter.

"You're so fucking agile, you get into everything."

Blue eyes sparkled against her chocolate coloring.

"I'm not happy with you." I shook my finger, but she merely sauntered along the edge of the stove. The more she ignored me, the madder I got.

"You can't do this. Bad!"

But nothing registered with my cat.

I scooped trash into my hand. Anger welled inside me like a flash of heat that had no beginning or end. It was all consuming.

"She should listen to you."

Don't you think I know that?

I grabbed the brush and dustpan beneath the kitchen sink, but instead of sweeping crap into the pan, I swung the brush like a bat and knocked Bonita off the oven. She sailed into the air and skimmed along the floor on her side. When she finally came to a stop, sapphire eyes flashed at me before she scurried away.

"Yeah, run away." I kicked the trash into the corner.

"Bye, Felicia."

You're a dick.

Quoting a movie line, albeit funny, wasn't helpful.

The stench and smallness of the kitchen closed in on me. I grabbed a beer from the refrigerator and fired up my laptop. Journaling would allow me to handle this better.

A Killer's Journal

The darkness seemed all too familiar when I first entered it. Memories of the not-so-

distant past always returned to remind me how utterly useless I was. At first I was afraid of the darkness. The vast emptiness and silence of it all frightened me.

I remember the times our babysitter, Brad, locked my twin brother and me in the closet knowing we were horrified of the dark. He was a dick, and we weren't even in school yet. But who were we to say something? Besides, if we had, my mom would've taken the blame, and my father would not only have allowed it, he would've added to her shame. And where would that have gotten us?

Now when I look back at my five-year-old self trapped in that dark closet, I don't view this encounter as fear but rather a way of embracing the darkness. And there was so much darkness.

The darkness was filled with hatred and fear. I hated Brad for putting us in the closet, and fear consumed me that my mom would leave us with him forever. Anytime she left, hatred and fear filled me until it felt like I would choke. Over time, I realized that those emotions weren't meant to be rejected but rather embraced. At first, I was *afraid of the loneliness of the darkness, but as I reflect on it now, I learned a lot from that experience.*

When fear is removed, the darkness isn't so dark and the alternative becomes freedom. Embracing a world where insecurities and fears are nonexistent allows the only thing that matters to emerge. And the only thing that matters is the preservation of one's self and one's desires.

I remember one time when my brother and I were with a friend. This was when we lived in a rural part of Wyoming. Our friend's family owned a feed store that sold animal feed and other farm shit. We were at his store after school, and his mom tasked us with the duty of searching, hunting, and killing any mice we could find.

Adrenaline pumped through my body at the idea. For once I was able to kill without the fear and repercussions I would face when confronted by others. The darkness inside me was allowed to come to the surface and take a breath.

This duty of finding mice was one I wouldn't

stray from. The challenge of exterminating these creatures was something I embraced. Are you beginning to see the connection? When you let go of fear, the darkness can surface.

In the beginning, we searched under old plywood and shipping containers to discover the infestation of these dirty creatures.

Over time, however, I separated from the group, as the thrill for the kill was too invigorating. I needed a scene of my own to perfect these masterpieces.

At first, I killed the mice with simple caveman-like tactics like stabbing and beating them with a thick stick until they died. However, it didn't take long before I tried all sorts of new ways to captivate my prey in order to keep me interested.

At one point, I filled a gallon-sized bucket with water and dropped the mice individually inside it to watch them struggle in order to preserve their life.

Their struggle immediately caught my attention. I was mesmerized by their desperate but futile skirmish. Their struggle to survive was primal. This I knew firsthand.

Before I could write my name, I learned that when my mom placed me in the empty dryer and my twin brother in the empty washing machine with the lids open that it was a form of survival. Hidden in the cavern with the door ajar, we knew my raging, fists-throwing father wouldn't find us.

But he always found her. I know now that she sacrificed herself for us. We were her weakness. What would've happened if she didn't have us to protect? Would she have left? Would she have survived?

I'll never know. Besides, what did it really matter? My mom was as helpless as the trapped mice that gasped and clawed at the sides of the bucket as if they had a chance. They never had a chance, and neither did she. To survive in this world, you save no one but yourself. Everyone is fair game.

And why not? Everyone in life attempts to live it the best way they can. Whether this means a nice house, nice car, a sexy wife, beautiful kids, everyone in this ever-so-boring, self-centered life is focused on making their lives so great that when death comes around, they can say they lived life to the fullest.

What I'm interested in is taking this so-called precious life of theirs and shortening it long before they live out their childish dreams. I learned a long time ago to let go of childish dreams. Dreams aren't a reality any more than happily ever after. It just doesn't exist. Not in my family and definitely not in my life.

Someone who doesn't realize that all lives are pointless and meaningless doesn't deserve to live in this world. Whatever you say or do to preserve and advance your life can all be pointless in a matter of seconds. Like the mice in the bucket.

People shouldn't be looking forward to living a long life but rather be concerned about the short life they already have.

I'm sickened and disgusted by those looking to preserve their lives beyond that of a normal person. This attempt at life is a futile and endless struggle that will *ultimately lead to nothingness. It is my duty to show these people that life is as sweet as it is short. Just like the mice. I was given that responsibility for a reason.*

If anyone were to read this, they would perceive my duty as a crime against life itself.

I personally believe I'm saving these self-righteous assholes who believe their lives are more important than everyone else's. They need to see the reality that they can die just as easily as anyone else, and therefore they are no one special at all. You can't really enjoy life until you've tasted the fear of death.

When my mom was pushed down the stairs, it was my sister's twin brother, Christopher, who bled out of her. By the age of five, I knew just how short my life was and just how much my father controlled the outcome.

My earliest memories are of fear. The fear that my father would find me. The fear that his rage would channel through his fists and sucker punch me like I'd seen him do to my mom. The fear that my body would cave in like a wounded bird like my mom's. Her arms came up like wings trying to protect herself, which only made him laugh. He actually laughed. It was a game. Our survival amused him.

At first, the darkness and emptiness were something I feared, but over time, I embraced it. I did not need the feelings of others; rather, I realized the potential I had and what I could do without those who burdened me. There were many thoughts and feelings I had when I first decided to act the way I felt was right, but over time I realized the faults of my ways. For me to really fit in society, I needed to persuade my peers, my parents, and every teacher I'd ever had that there was no fault in me. I was the kid next door. I fit in better than anyone. By assimilating to their life and their rules, I lived my own private life in the darkness with David beside me. David was my protector then as he is now.

Now, when a teacher or college professor tries to school me, it's my duty to teach them the lessons I've learned.

I saved the journal to the flash drive and then deleted the

file from my computer. I scrolled to the tab I'd bookmarked earlier and reviewed the blog post.

The online instructions provided a list of supplies and a step-by-step blueprint for making a dart gun. There wasn't anything on the supply list I hadn't been able to pick up at the dollar store on my way to the apartment.

All the necessary materials I bought were on my bed.

My mom once told me that the first item on an ingredient list was the most important. I didn't know if that was true, but it made sense that PVC pipe topped the supply list. It wasn't big, only six inches, but it was big enough to do what I wanted. Besides the pipe, I had a female PVC coupling, a laser pointer, electrical tape, a Styrofoam ring to hold the nail darts, wall nails, sticky notes, zip ties, and permanent glue.

After attaching the coupling to the end of the pipe, I slid the Styrofoam ring midway down the pipe until it was positioned just above where I'd secure the laser pointer. I carefully wrapped the white PVC pipe and Styrofoam dart holder in black electrical tape. A red zip tie secured the laser pointer in place. All that was left to make were the darts.

I placed a nail in the corner of a sticky note and rolled the paper until it created a funnel top. I trimmed the excess paper so each nail had a coned top, which would catch air better. I secured the cone in place with glue, then repeated this process with more than a dozen nails.

I stuck the makeshift darts into the Styrofoam holder, which made them easier to grab.

I was ready for a practice shot.

I glanced around my apartment. Bonita's tail swayed from behind the blinds.

For better accuracy, I sighted the red laser on her tail. I quietly pushed a nail into the coupler of the pipe so that when I blew, air would fill the paper cone and send the nail dart soaring toward my target.

I sealed my lips around the pipe and blew hard. The nail dinged Bonita, who screamed and darted away, but it didn't pierce her the way I'd hoped.

Maybe I needed sharper nails.

"No!"

David's voice was strong today.

"You just need to blow harder."

The joke was on the tip of my tongue, but I could tell he wasn't in a playful mood.

"Listen, that professor of yours is a real asshole. People like that need to disappear."

"This dart gun won't kill them," I said to him.

"But in the right spot, it could definitely scar them."

His voice was louder than mine lately.

"Get 'em in the eye or throat. Try again."

This time I filled my lungs with air, sealed my mouth even tighter around the coupling, and blew hard. The nail zipped through the air and into the wall.

"Nice."

Thanks. But how do you expect me to pull this off?

I searched my apartment for my cat, but Bonita was nowhere to be found.

The only way it could possibly work was if I sat in the

middle of the class surrounded by other students. I couldn't separate from the herd. But even then, how the fuck was this going to work?

"Every Monday they show a TED Talk. When the intro music for it starts and the professor is still at the front of the classroom, pull the dart gun out of your backpack."

Right. The music should drown the sound of me blowing into the pipe. And hopefully in the darkened room, no one would notice.

"Aim for the throat or the eye. Leave a mark."

Don't you think that's a little harsh?

"Don't be a pussy. Do you think that jerk deserves mercy?"

No, they don't.

I packed my backpack for class, carefully tucking my dart gun into the front pocket. I just wanted to scare them. Nothing harmful, just a little zap to tell the blowhard who was really in charge.

Sundays usually sucked, but now I couldn't wait for the night to end so the fun could begin.

CHAPTER 21

BRANSON

THE soundtrack for *Titanic* played from the apartment across from the hall. For once the heater worked in November, but it worked too well. When the windows in my apartment started to steam, I opened the door. It was Sunday night, and I missed Hope. We spent the Sunday together until I had to drive back for Monday classes. She told me she didn't like to be alone, so next semester I'd only take Tuesday-Thursday classes so I could spend Sunday night with her. Or maybe I could take my last semester online. There was something about Hope that made me want to reach the finish line for college as quickly as possible. The sooner I did, the sooner I could be with her on a full-time basis and not this weekends-only bullshit. Until then I was stuck in Casper while Hope was in Cheyenne.

The end of a weekend was universally felt on campus. I learned early on that in this apartment complex, whatever hookups happened on Friday were either fizzling or reaching new heights by this point. From the sickeningly slow beat of "My Heart Will Go On" and its melodramatic lyrics, it sounded like things were on a high note for my neighbor. I had two choices: suffer through the kill-me-now music or drop my last ten pounds through sweat.

Bob from the Depression Center would probably want to move into the building if he knew how scorching they kept the apartments. We now Snapchatted, and anytime his story popped up on my phone, I laughed. The cat was funny as hell and painfully honest.

I grabbed my phone, slid down the side of the couch facing the front door and the only notable breeze, and called Aaron.

"Jeffrey," he answered.

"Fucker." I shook my head and was pretty sure sweat flung from my scalp. "It's Africa hot in here."

"Stop your whining. Least you don't have to pay for heat," he said. "I just got my electric bill, and it was sixty bucks. Can you believe that shit?"

"What? Is sixty a lot for heat?" I honestly didn't know.

"Sure, if it was for a month's worth of heat, that'd be awesome, but this was for last month's air conditioning, and I only had the AC on for a few days."

"That's a bummer."

"Yeah, I'm going to see if Mom can help me out."

"Dude, you're joking, right?" I said with a laugh. "Mom's got a lot going on right now. Hope and I brought her soup last time I was in town. The chemo's hitting her hard."

"Yeah, I know. I talk to her. But I'm not getting paid

shit on or off campus. I'm making $8.50 an hour at three different jobs."

"Three jobs? I thought you worked at the library and the grocery store. Did you get *another* job?" I asked.

"No. Well, yeah, kind of. It's my internship at the nonprofit."

"How's that going?" I stretched my legs, and the sweat under my knees left a watermark on the carpet.

"It's a shit show. Our building homes event is our biggest deal of the year, and my executive board is a joke."

"Executive board? Are they paid?"

Aaron blew a raspberry into the receiver. "No, they're not paid, and neither am I."

"Then why do it?" It seemed obvious to me—no pay, no work.

"Bran, it's good on a résumé. I'm the president of the executive board that helps build homes. What sucks is the other people on the board. They're total morons. I'll say, 'Hey, do this,' and they need step-by-step directions. So I'll ask them to do the simplest job, like get twelve dozen bagels for the build. Not hard. Or go get hot water from the student union so we can have bagels and coffee for our volunteer home builders. But instead of doing it, I get a text from Mike at six thirty that he couldn't get the water and the union closes at seven. So I had to go all the way back to the union and get the water for these massive coffeepots. Then fuckin' Jill brings nine dozen bagels, not twelve, nine. And then our finance chair, Jayla, didn't print the Excel sheets that listed what all the volunteers were doing that night."

"Quit," I said. "That's bullshit. Just quit."

"You can't quit a volunteer job. Besides, I've worked too hard this semester to have it fall apart now. But I want to say, 'Do you guys even give a shit?'"

"When's it over? Your term," I said.

"We have one more house build before Christmas, and then I'm finished."

"And then what, you're just done?"

"Then the vice chair, Chad, who's a total cunt, takes over in January. This guy can't even come to our mandatory exec meetings but has his dad, who's the vice president of the bank and a college alum, email me because I gave his kid a hard time for not making the meetings. His father's a cunt too."

"Bro, you're making my head hurt with all this shit."

It was good to hear my brother laugh. He always took things so seriously.

"Nah, it's fine. I mean, none of them got me their transition guides, and I'm like good luck running it next semester. Fuck you. If they all died, I'd be at the funeral doing a tap dance on their coffins."

The next thing I heard was the sound of rapping on a table.

"I'd just tap the shit outta their coffins," he said after he concluded his impromptu tap. "Buh-bye, suckers."

The change in his voice along with the tapping made me laugh even more.

"So if anyone were to ask you in a job interview, 'How was your home building experience?' how'd you respond?"

I asked, knowing Aaron would deliver something funny.

"Fuck. That. Shit." He laughed again. "Let everyone go homeless. It's easier."

I chuckled.

"And what really gets me is that everyone on the board is like 'You complain too much.' And all I can think is 'You want to be in my shoes for a day?' I swear to God, Branson, you'd punch someone. But thankfully I'm almost finished with this semester."

"I wouldn't be messed up in that volunteer bullshit to begin with," I said, and we both started snickering all over again.

"Bro, I'm not kidding you, this semester I had a permanent twitch. When people would say, 'How's it going?' I'd go, 'Uh, yeah, really good.'" The shift in his voice was funny as hell.

If I wasn't already sitting on the floor, my side-splitting laughter would've had me there in a heartbeat.

Then his voice shifted once again and his tone became much more serious. "I don't know. It's like a sign of respect. This entire year has been hell on me. I don't like the fact that I get disrespected so often by my executive board. I can't be mad at them, so I have to put on this face like it's okay while they just go on disrespecting me."

"Uh, I don't know if it's really disrespect so much as stupidity and laziness," I said, thinking back to the Depression Center and the piece on accepting the shit we can't change. "People say the most fucked-up things to me all the time, and I'm learning that it's just ignorance. I'd love to tell people to back the fuck off and check their assumptions about me, but all that'll do is make them think I'm crazier than I am."

"Like that sorority bitch at the community college," he said, and I shrugged.

"She actually had reason to question my sanity." I chuckled. "But in the long run, she's not worth my time."

"Yeah, and from the pic you showed me in church, looks like someone put her in check."

I grimaced. "Yeah, I dunno. I haven't thought about her."

"I get where you're coming from, Branson, but you can't let people disrespect you."

"She's stupid. If her opinion actually mattered to me, then yeah, it probably would've bothered me more, but she's no one to me." It was always weird whenever I heard this inner truth come out of me that I didn't even realize was there. But it was true. That girl meant nothing to me. It seemed to bother my brother more than it bothered me.

"Whatever, bro. It's your life."

"Harsh," I said, which was only met by silence.

When he finally did speak again, he wrapped back to a neutral topic. "So yeah, working two menial jobs and then interning for free, I'm fucked when my AC bill is an extra sixty bucks."

I nodded. "Understood. I'm just not sure now's the time to ask Mom, you know?"

"Listen, I've got to go."

I knew my brother as well as I knew myself. His quick exit was a less-than-subtle fuck you. Whatever. I knew everything would be back to normal by tomorrow.

CHAPTER 22

DAVID AND ME

I never understood the crowd mentality. I'd seen it at school, concerts, and hell, even the grocery store on Black Friday. Everyone huddled outside waiting for the doors to open, and as soon as they did, instead of separating from the group, everyone followed the pack into the same section until it filled up. Only then did they realize they had to find their own path. What I didn't get were the dumbass blank expressions on the followers' faces when section A in the stadium was filled, which of course left B through Z available, but don't tell the sheep that. They'd rather bleat and wander aimlessly, waiting for a new herd to follow.

It was social proof that at the core, people weren't born leaders but born followers. Instead of finding their own way, tapping into their own resources, they simply fell in line with the crowd.

I'd never been a follower. I wasn't saying I was a leader, but I did pave my own way.

So it was really fucked up when I fell in line behind the herd of students and sat beside them in the center section of the auditorium versus my normal seat away from everyone.

It pissed me off because today I had a choice. That hadn't always been the case. From my earliest recollections, I'd always been singled out, whether it was from my dad when he got angry or my mom's reliance upon me to be her emotional support. I'd never been just a part of anything before.

If it were still the caveman days, my exclusion from the fold would've meant death. And in some ways, my role in the family did just that. I was singled out for not being more of what they needed.

I'd never forget the summer before college. I worked at the golf course where my old man was head of the pro shop. I missed one day of work, and when he came home yelling, I sensed things wouldn't go well. When he repeatedly tapped his finger into my sternum, calling me a bitch and a pussy, I did the one thing that was unforgivable: I cried.

The pressure of his finger increased until I felt my chest collapse. When it hurt to breathe and I couldn't catch my breath, he stopped. Later that night, his girlfriend took me to urgent care. After the X-rays, they asked me how I'd fractured my sternum. For a second, I thought about telling the truth, but I knew better. My survival was dependent on maintaining the lie. Besides, telling the truth would isolate me further in the family. And especially from my father, who'd deny that he had anything to do with it anyway. In my father's world, his reality was all that mattered.

Four years later, my dissention from my family was complete and 100 percent self-imposed. Why wait until they cut me out of their lives?

"Fuck that."

Agreed.

I took control of my life and stopped hoping for that *someday* when my family would see me as something other than my siblings' keeper.

It helped that David and I created our own pack. Of course, my twin brother didn't know about David. I knew he'd never judge me, but like Trevor, he'd want David gone. And he'd be more than happy to tell me that David wasn't real. He'd throw around buzzwords like "command hallucination," "psychotic episode," or maybe go as far as "psychotic break." The people those terms impacted were the caregivers. When a command hallucination took charge, a caregiver's life disappeared. I couldn't really blame them. Who wanted to have their life upended?

But on the flipside—and let's be honest, no one ever considered the flipside—the people in my life didn't understand what it was like with David. If they did, they'd know that all it boiled down to was jealousy. No one liked Trevor because of the time and attention his presence took away from my greedy little family. Don't get me wrong, I didn't like Trevor, but I was never jealous of him. David and Trevor may not have been *real* people, but it begged the question…

"What is real?"

Exactly.

Was it following everyone else in the guise of social harmony? I lived the first twenty years of my life keeping the peace and copying the behavior of others to fit in. It got me nowhere. I remained the outsider. *There are no shortcuts to acceptance—you're either in or out.* Whether you were "in" or "out" may have been some cute little catchphrase on those reality TV shows, but when it was your own life, it wasn't so cute to be the one on the outside always looking in.

So there I was, forced to assimilate in order to do what I had to do. Even though there was an empty seat on either side of me in the classroom, I felt boxed in. A dude with more arm hair than Sasquatch was on one side of me, and a girl who smelled as strong and fruity as one of the bath stores I hurried past in the mall so I wouldn't suffocate from the stench was on the other side. I sat amongst the crowd in the lecture hall with students beside me, behind me, and in front of me. I practically felt their breath on my cheeks and neck.

"Fucking people."

Agreed.

"Mr. Kovak." The professor gave a nod toward my new placement in class.

I gave the customary nod in return. Just another sheep in the fold. Bleat, bleat, bleat.

"Would you care to share your takeaway from the chapter that was assigned?"

"Fuck that."

I sat where I did to fit *in*, not stand out. "Nah, I'm good."

The dude next to me laughed, and the girl who bathed in perfume muttered, "I don't think it was a request," under her breath.

I rolled my eyes and waited. If the professor wanted me to give the highlights of the chapter, then they should tell me, not ask. Ask any college senior if they wanted to share anything and the likely answer would be an emphatic no. No, I didn't want to share my thoughts on any chapter. No, I didn't want to be in the class. And hell no to the feigned look of concern on the professor's face.

"No. No. No."

Exactly my thought.

My ass was in the room. That was enough.

"Would *anyone* like to share the highlights of the chapter before we begin today's TED Talk?"

Thankfully no one, not even the do-gooders in the very front row, volunteered to bore us with a recap.

"Perhaps you'll have comments after the TED talk." The professor moved toward the computer and began pressing buttons. Two screens slowly descended from the ceiling.

I reached into my backpack, which was tucked beside the empty seat next to the stinky girl, and held the tip of the dart gun. While it remained hidden from sight, I kept waiting for an adrenaline spike or shaky hands, but neither happened. Instead, I felt nothing.

David was right. The professor deserved this. I was simply carrying out what they deserved. I rapped my foot on the concrete floor, waiting for the lights to darken.

The dual screens went from white to color within a

matter of seconds. The red "TED" logo flashed in the top left corner of each screen. The introductory music was next, which was my cue.

The lights in the lecture hall went from bright to dark so quickly that it allowed me to slide the dart gun from my bag to my mouth without anyone seeing me. Everyone was too busy adjusting their focus to the screens that flashed "TED" in red. Everyone fell in line the way I knew they would.

A nail dart was already lodged in the gun. I couldn't use the laser because the red beam would draw attention to me, so instead I just aimed toward the podium where the professor stood beside the computer, drew in a deep, strong breath, and blew—*hard*. The coned dart sailed through the front two rows and struck the professor perfectly in their backside.

A small yelp followed, and the professor quickly turned around.

I casually leaned forward like I was tying my shoe and tipped my backpack so it fell to the floor. I slid the dart gun back inside the bag just as the lights flashed on. My eyes were already adjusted, but I rubbed them anyway like I was trying to erase sleep from them. Really, I had to do something to prevent myself from laughing or staring or both.

David's plan worked.

The professor held up the nail dart.

"Would anyone like to claim this?"

"What is it?" someone in the front row asked.

"It appears to be a nail with paper wrapped around it,"

the professor said.

"Is there a note?" I asked, which prompted the professor to uncurl the paper and look for the nonexistent letter. I should've ended it there, but it was too perfect. "Maybe something you want to *share* with us?"

I'd heard the expression that someone's face drained of color, but I never knew if that was an actual thing or not. The professor's face lost all color, which wasn't a good look.

"Mr. Kovak." The professor's voice quaked.

"Yes?" Mine didn't.

"Would you care to explain this?" The professor held the nail dart higher.

I shrugged. "You said it was a nail with a paper wrapped around it." I squinted toward the podium. "I dunno. I thought maybe there was a note. Like someone was sending you a message."

"Dick move."

Was it?

Color slowly returned, but the professor's composure was off, like they were rattled or had PTSD. But instead of anger, the pained expression on the professor's face revealed one emotion—betrayal. I knew it well. It happened when I'd cried as my dad raged and stabbed me in the chest with his finger. I couldn't believe he'd unleash on me—only he had. And in doing so, he broke my trust.

"See. I knew you weren't ready for their reaction."

Whatever. I'm fine.

"Then why are you reliving what happened with your dad?"

Because he broke my trust. I trusted that my dad wouldn't hit me. Maybe when I was a defenseless kid, but not when I was a young adult about to go to college. My fractured sternum was nothing compared to how shattered my belief was that I mattered. I didn't matter—not to my dad or even in my family.

"You matter to me."

Thanks.

Still, betrayal was the one emotion that, by its very nature, blindsided even the most hardened hearts.

The professor's bowed head was something I also recognized. Most people would think the body language screamed of shame, but shame was accepting blame for someone else's actions—something I'd learned when I was little and my mom moved us into a shelter for battered women. We had to attend all these family counseling sessions.

"A lot of good that did."

Agreed.

No, the professor's lowered head was from defeat. Not in the same sense as being defeated in a video game—this was real defeat which equated to real loss. It was what happened when trust was broken. The loss was great. Nothing was more devastating or lonelier than broken trust.

The professor directed their next comments toward the ground.

"We're ending early today." Nothing more was said. The professor turned and walked toward the emergency exit.

I waited for a triumphant surge to course through me to

invigorate my senses, but it never came. As everyone filed behind each other to exit the class, I fell in line and felt nothing.

CHAPTER 23

DAVID AND ME

I'D always heard that the definition of insanity was repeating the same behavior and expecting a different result. But something didn't click with the dart gun. There was no high afterward, not even a little.

In a bold move, I pulled a Britney and shaved my head. I get why she did it. It's freeing. I once read that Britney Spears shaved her luscious locks to strip herself of her sexuality. I didn't buy it. It was all the crap you battled, day after day, month after month for years that finally reached its apex. To the naked eye, it looked like she snapped when really the girl was tired of being a puppet. I totally got it. Sometimes, the most shocking acts were the sanest.

My phone chimed with a text that my Uber driver was five minutes away from the apartment. I slung my black ski bag over my shoulder, tucked the fake ID into the front of my wallet, and was about to lock the door behind me when I remembered the bag with my disassembled dart gun.

I grabbed the bag and was locking the door when a voice hit my ear.

"Wow, check you out."

I turned around. A neighbor I barely exchanged hellos with was right outside my door. The dude was in my bubble.

"Thanks. Thought it was time to mix things up."

He chuckled. "Respect. Not sure I'd go into the winter with a shaved head, but"—he shrugged—"it'll save time in the morning."

I nodded.

"You headed to the mountains?" He nodded toward my ski bag.

"As soon as they open."

"Huh." The guy seemed fixated on the bag.

"Fucker."

Agreed.

I elbowed my bag. "Yeah, picking up new alpine skis."

When he didn't seem convinced, I told him the truth. "Actually," I said, leaning toward him, "I ordered an Uber so I can go buy a rifle. You know, something small like an AK-47."

"Sure." The guy laughed. "You get the guns and I'll line up the dope."

"Next time," I said, heading toward the stairwell. I wasn't about to take the elevator and have to deal with someone else.

"Fucking people."

I know, right?

I passed the dumpster on my way to the Uber and

chucked the remnants of the dart gun into the trash before tossing the bag in as well. I separated them on purpose. People got caught because they were stupid.

"You're anything but stupid."

Precisely my point.

Both Ohio and Wyoming allowed people to openly carry firearms without any state permit. Anyone twenty-one years or older could openly carry a weapon. Neither state required a universal background check at the point of sale either, unless I was stupid and bought it from a licensed firearm dealer. But like David reminded me, I wasn't stupid.

When my Uber driver pulled alongside the pawn shop, a credit card linked to a prepaid debit card paid my fare. For anyone interested, David Ducharme took an Uber from the college apartments to the pawn shop.

I hopped out of the car and headed toward the pawn shop that was sketchy as fuck. It was in one of those strip malls beside other random shops that sold useless shit like rugs, lamps, and lightbulbs. There was even a VCR repair shop.

"What the hell?"

I scoffed, agreeing.

I opened the door and bells rang.

"Jesus. Bells? What is this, church?"

I grinned.

"Be right with you," a male voice said from the depths of the store. The place was huge, like a bulk store for people's castaways.

"It's okay, Pedro, I've got it." An Asian woman who was probably a few years older than me approached the counter. "Is there something I can help you find?"

Her super-short blue hair matched her eyes. A black scarf was tied around her slender neck, and big hoop earrings dangled onto her narrow shoulders. She had on a white thermal and black leggings and wore both exceptionally well. She reminded me of someone so much that I found myself staring at her.

"Looking for skis?" she said.

"Oh, uh, not really." I felt heat rush to my face, so I quickly glanced toward the tower of DVDs on the wall behind her. A stack of anime movies caught my attention, which was when it hit me. I returned my focus to her and stared into eyes that were as blue as the ocean and just as deep. "Has anyone told you that you look like Bulma from *Dragonball Z*?"

When she smiled, dimples appeared on each side of her face. "Yeah, I've heard that."

"You an anime fan?" I asked.

"If you pick the right year, yeah."

That did more than pique my curiosity. It flat-out wooed me. "I'm a fan of *One Piece*, early 2000s."

She grinned. "*Fairy Tale* is more my style, 2009."

I shook my head. "Nah, doesn't count. The first season is *always* the best."

Her entire face and parts of her neck turned red. "Okay, *Korea Boo*, then, 2014."

I laughed. "*Korea Boo*? Good try. Those are *Japanese* anime."

"Just checking if you knew the difference," she said.

I stole a quick glance at her name tag, which was upside down. All I could make out was that it began with a K—or maybe it ended with a K—and had a lot of vowels in between.

"Are you Japanese?" Asking someone their ethnicity wasn't something I normally did. But neither was taking an Uber to a pawn shop to buy a gun. It seemed to be a day of firsts.

"Well, at least you didn't ask if I was Chinese, Japanese, or my favorite, Asian. Or better still, where I'm *really* from."

"I don't even know where to start. First off, I apologize if I was rude."

"You weren't," she said. "You were actually straightforward, and I appreciate that. I'm Korean." She flipped her name tag around.

"Katie?"

"I was adopted."

"Cool."

Her dimples appeared again. "Is it?" She shook her head and shades of blue swooshed back and forth. "My name is as American as it gets."

I shrugged. "It's a stupid cultural thing Americans do—we either name our kids after ourselves or someone we want to impress."

She laughed.

"I gotta tell ya, I'm still stuck on the Asian thing. People really ask if you're Asian?"

"*All* the time."

"Don't they realize that Asia is an umbrella for multiple ethnicities and geographies? Are they total morons?"

"Yes," she said with a chuckle. "They usually are. Or they ask if I'm Asian American, as if I can only be from one particular place."

"I'm sorry." It was all I knew to say.

"It's okay. After you've been asked what kind of Asian you are, you learn tricks to mess with them."

I leaned toward the counter that separated us and got a hint of honeysuckle-scented perfume. "Such as…?"

"When someone asks where I'm from, I tell them that I'm from Utah and then ask where they're from."

I laughed. "Oh shit. What happens?"

"There's usually this pause like they're really confused. Because clearly someone who looks like me could *not* be from America. So of course they press." Her eyes narrowed when she spoke. "'No, where are you *really* from?' they ask. As if Utah couldn't possibly be my home state."

I shook my head, which would've looked better if I still had hair. "That's bullshit. No one's really American. We all migrated here or were forcibly brought here. We're all immigrants of some sort. America is too young a country to pull that card. Older countries are smarter. In China there are more than *fifty* ethnic groups. If the US ever conducted an honest census, I'd bet money there are hundreds of thousands of ethnic groups thriving in our country that just aren't recognized." I paused and took a step off my soapbox. "Sorry." I paused again. "I'm in my last year of college, and current events are really all I get excited about anymore.

And I tend to get a little crazy when I hear stupid shit."

"No apology necessary. It's refreshing. Most people don't know their own state, let alone the geography or history of another one. I don't mind if people ask me, like you did, if I'm Japanese or Korean or, hell, from outer space. I'll answer a direct question, no problem. It's when they follow it by telling me how much they like pad thai, which *isn't* a Korean food, and even if it was, why tell me? What does that have to do with anything? Somehow who I am reminds them of a meal? It's not like I go up to Americans and say, 'Hey, I like hamburgers and fries. Nice to meet you.'"

I laughed. Her candor was invigorating. She was a stunner both physically and mentally. I knew I had to bring my A-game, which included a healthy dose of realism. "In four years of college, I've learned one thing—people are stupid."

She giggled.

"Do you speak Korean?" I asked, and her blue eyes practically danced.

"No one ever asks me that. I wish I did, but I left Korea when I was six months old, and my parents only speak English."

When I didn't comment, she smiled again.

"So you're not going to ask me how much they paid to get me?"

Shocked, nervous laughter escaped me. "Jesus, no. What the fuck?"

"If I'm not grilled about where I'm from, which shuts some people down when I don't give them the answer they want, what *always* holds their interest is when someone finds out I was adopted." She leaned her elbows on the glass counter and barely took up any space. "Adoption brings up a whole new round of questions, like how much my parents bought me for."

I rolled my eyes. "Seriously, like I said, people are stupid." I scratched the back of my head, which was usually covered with hair.

"Trying to get ahead of a receding hairline?" she asked with a flip of her chin toward me.

"How'd you guess?" I palmed my scalp and stubble moved back and forth across my fingers.

"So, baldy, what can I help you find today?"

Suddenly the reality of why I was there didn't press on me with the same intensity as it had when I left. But David did.

"Buy the gun."

I shook my head and scanned the contents of the glass-enclosed counter. Rings. Pocket watches. Knives. My focus returned to the rings.

"Could I see that ruby ring?" I tapped the glass with my finger.

"Excellent choice," she said.

"It's not what you think." I smiled. "My mom's...."

"Don't be the pathetic loser with the sick mom."

"My brother and I got my mom this really awful fake ruby ring for Mother's Day once, and I've always wanted to make it right."

"Ahhh."

I purposefully exaggerated my eye roll. "If you saw what we gave her, you'd understand."

"I bet it was perfect." She unlocked the glass cabinet and fished out the ring, then handed it to me.

"Well fuck, if you aren't going to get a gun, at least have the balls to ask her out."

"Uh." I shook my head and stared at the red stone. "There's a really dope anime conference in California that I was thinking of going to." I glanced up into her blue eyes. "Road-tripping with another anime nerd would make the trip a thousand times better."

Before she could reject my offer, a dude in a camo jacket approached. "Hey, babe, need help with anything?"

"Pedro, I was just showing…." Her face and neck blotched red. "I forgot to get your name."

I shrugged. "David. I'm David."

She grinned. "David was interested in getting his mom a ring."

It sounded as pathetic as David warned me it would. I instantly handed her back the ring and directed my attention to Pedro. "Actually, I was hoping to look at your guns."

CHAPTER 24

DAVID AND ME

THE 30 percent chance of thunderstorms turned into 100 percent rain. Still, instead of being dropped off directly in front of my apartment, I had the Uber driver return me to another spot on campus. Even though he was a completely different driver, why risk it? Besides, rain or not, the front stone arch that welcomed everyone to the university was dope.

E Pluribus Unum was etched beneath the university's name in the gray-colored stone. During orientation, it was explained that the Latin motto meant "out of many, one." It was adopted by the Founding Fathers for the seal that's on all our money. The idea was that out of many states, one country was formed. It was as American as it got.

It also fit my mood.

Out of all the many pawn shops, I'd picked the one with a newlywed couple who were cash poor and needed to sell stuff. It sucked that Katie was married, but it totally explained her personality. Married women flirted more than women who weren't. It was like they knew the signal they sent off could never be returned, so it created this safe space for them to be as forward as they wanted. Either that or they were bored as fuck and wanted to flirt with total strangers to spice shit up in their lives. Didn't matter. Katie was married to Pedro. And Pedro was one dude I wouldn't fuck with. His camo jacket did little to disguise that the guy was ripped.

I slung my ski bag over my shoulder, and the weight of the rifle rested against my back. The box of bullets bumped against my thigh with each step.

Students ran through the quad with backpacks over their heads as if they'd melt from the light splattering of rain.

"Lame."

Agreed.

The mass amount of people running all around campus didn't even bother me. I was at peace. I had a plan, one that would get the results David wanted. I wasn't crazy about it, but if it meant David and I were on the same page, I'd do it.

Thunder cracked and lightning lit the sky. More students blurred past me, but the rain and I kept a steady pace. I headed toward the student union for a bite to eat and glanced in the direction of my apartment complex. A campus cop car was parked on the side of the building beside the dumpsters. I kept walking toward the union with my focus on my upstairs apartment. I had a corner apartment that was easy to spot from a distance, even through the rain. But to see my front door, I walked diagonally, away from the union and closer toward the complex, to get a clearer view.

My front door was shut, but someone stood off to the side.

"What the fuck?"

Yeah, what's up with that?

I squinted just as a campus cop popped up from the side stairwell. He walked in the direction of the other dude, who was outside my apartment.

"Tom? Is that Tom?"

It looked like my resident advisor, but I couldn't be sure.

My stomach tightened and I clenched my jaw. It felt like I'd been hit by one of the lightning bolts that broke through the gray clouds. My heart raced, and even though it was raining, I felt sweat running down my leg. Either that or I'd pissed myself.

"Stay calm and hide the gun."

David's voice in my head was the only one that drowned out all others.

The university was a stone's throw—or gun toss—away from the biggest river in the state. I walked toward the north end of campus and the footbridge that overlooked the river. The light rain became a downpour. The sudden high-pitched, ear-splitting sound of the tornado siren startled me, and I flinched. My entire body tensed so much that my muscles cramped when I walked.

"Keep it together. This is no time to look suspicious. Man up."

My measured steps were a stark contrast to other students who zigzagged across campus through the onslaught of rain. I held on to the strap of the ski bag and began to jog toward the footbridge. It was mid-November, and I silently prayed to whoever would still listen to me that there wasn't any ice on the river. The footbridge was the fastest way to cross the river or, in my case, dump something into it.

"Hide it."

No.

I never should've bought the gun. My bald head felt every pelt of rain like God's wrath hailing down on me.

The sirens continued to sound, warning everyone to take shelter from the impending tornado. I ignored them and kept moving. Gloomy, heavy clouds covered the sky, and night replaced day like someone had flipped a switch and turned out all the lights. Suddenly, I was in the dark.

"I'm here. It's okay."

But it didn't feel okay. My eyes burned, and I just wanted to hold someone's hand. Worse still, David's voice wasn't reassuring me. I was alone.

Blinking until my eyes adjusted to the dark, I then focused on the lights that softly illuminated the bridge in the distance.

But if I could see the bridge, wouldn't the campus cops be able to see me? If they were at my apartment, wouldn't they be looking for me?

"Pussy."

My jaw tightened.

Shut up.

"Your dad's right, you are a bitch."

Shut up. Shut up. Shut up!

I walked as fast as I dared, as the path that led to the

footbridge was well worn and slippery from the rain. I took the stairs that led to the bridge's entrance two at a time. Other students and faculty were ahead of me on the bridge; I hung back until there was enough distance between me and the last person on the bridge to go unnoticed.

I unzipped the ski bag and removed the rifle as easily and unsuspiciously as I would skis. The most obvious things were done in the open. If I acted weird, people would notice. If I didn't, they wouldn't care.

I glanced behind me. The next herd of people approached the steps. It was either throw the rifle now or never. I walked briskly on the steel-grid deck, dropped the rifle like a piece of trash over the side, and kept walking. My $300 cash purchase disappeared in the dark, fast-flowing river. I grabbed the box of bullets, ripped the top off, and let its contents fall like silver confetti over the side of the bridge. I was about to toss my ski bag when David's voice in my head became a command.

"Keep it."

Why?

It made no sense. The campus cops were at my apartment. It had to be that nosey neighbor who saw me with my ski bag and freaked out when I said I was buying an AK-47. It was the only thing that made sense.

I ripped the airport tag off the handle of the bag so violently that I yanked myself forward and lost my balance. My feet slid out from beneath me on the slick grating, and no matter how hard I tried to regain my balance, I couldn't. The river rushed below me, and for a second I thought I'd end up in it. I held out my hand to break my fall, and in the process my ski bag fell from my shoulder into the river. I landed flat on my ass, still gripping the bag tag.

I glanced over my shoulder to see the group of students was now on the bridge. I began to stand, though every muscle in my body hurt. All I had left to dump was my fake ID. I grabbed my wallet and David's driver's license that was in front of mine and sent it flying into the night like a Frisbee. David would not be pleased, which was more terrifying than anything that had happened all night.

CHAPTER 25

DAVID AND ME

NOW that the rifle was gone, as well as any evidence of who purchased it, I was in the clear. Hell, I was like the tornado that roared through town and left just as quickly—virtually untraceable. So I wasn't sure why I hesitated to go to my apartment. I stood in the shadows of the complex and watched. There hadn't been any activity for more than an hour, but the campus cop car was still parked outside. I didn't think anyone went inside my apartment, but there was no way to know until I went inside. My resident advisor, Tom, had a key, but he wouldn't just go into my apartment, would he?

"Is that even legal?"

I don't know.

I quickly googled student housing rights and found a shit ton of blogs on the topic. The takeaway was threefold: remain calm, I didn't have to consent to a search, and *always* request an attorney. If they had a search warrant, chances were the search would continue without me. I was sure they were on the lookout for some kind of contraband. But David and I both knew that wasn't what they'd find.

"Why are you freaking out?"

Oh, I don't know. Maybe because there's a cop outside my apartment.

"Get a grip. Don't be such a pussy."

I'm not. I'm just assessing the situation.

Everyone on campus knew that the university hired local police officers to patrol the campus during the school year. They had arrest authority, which I didn't want to test.

Even if the cops didn't get involved, the university could still exercise its disciplinary rights, which usually meant that if I didn't comply with whatever they wanted, they could expel me.

It happened to a buddy of mine. He was accused of hacking the transcript office and wouldn't turn over his computer. I didn't know if the university didn't have enough evidence or not, only that when he refused their request for his computer, they kicked him off campus and out of school. I was sure there was more to the story than that, but I remembered him saying that the school had these clauses that protected them and screwed the students. They basically could do whatever they wanted.

"But expulsion?"

I know, right?

Four years of college with fifteen credits shy from graduating, and I could lose it all. It'd be one thing if they didn't let me graduate because I owed them money, which

I did. But to lose everything I'd worked so hard to earn just didn't seem right.

"It's bullshit and it's not fair."

You're right.

Adrenaline kicked in and I bolted toward the stairwell that led to my apartment. Tom and a scrawny cop stood off to the side. As soon as they spotted me, they briskly walked in the direction of my apartment.

"Hey, guys. How's it goin'?" I said as I approached.

The cop glanced at a piece of paper that had my photo on it and then back at me, but it was Tom who spoke.

"We'd like to talk," he said.

"Sure, what's up?"

"Perhaps we could go inside." Tom nodded to my apartment.

"I'd rather not." I grimaced. "It's kind of a mess."

"We don't mind," the cop said.

"But I do," I said resolutely, enforcing my fourth amendment rights.

"And without a warrant, you can't do dick, motherfuckers."

"Okay." Tom clapped his hands together. "I'll get right to the point. We were notified that you had made some dangerous-sounding comments that were concerning. With your permission, we'd like to search your apartment."

"If you're referring to the stoner who lives on this floor, he joked about buying dope and I joked about buying an AK-47." I held up my left hand like I was taking an oath. "Which I can now see was in poor taste. But that's all it was, a dumb comment."

"Sounds harmless enough. Let's just go inside and talk about this," Tom said.

The guy was good.

"No, we can talk here," I replied.

"The complaint mentioned a ski bag," Tom pressed.

Damn criminal justice major. Why can't he just go away?

I nodded. "Yup, I was thinking of buying new alpine skis."

"Where's the bag now?" the campus cop asked.

"In the river," I said and didn't blink at their shocked expressions. "I was on the footbridge headed to Poor Boy's Pub when it started dumping on me. Everyone was running, but when I did, I turfed it. My bag flew off my shoulder, and before I could get it, it slipped over the side and into the river." It was the truth, so I knew neither my face nor voice would betray me.

I turned my hands palm-side up and showed the burn marks from skidding on the grated bridge. They both took a quick yet inquisitive glance.

"It hurt like hell." I rubbed my palms on my jeans. "And that bag wasn't cheap. Some lucky bastard's going to find it next spring."

Tom wearily smiled like he was trying to get on board with my story. At this point, all he had was some stoner's version of what happened. I wasn't about to give him anything solid he could use.

"Whatever. When did talking about buying a gun become illegal?"

Shut up. That's the least of our troubles. You know why they're here.

"Listen, I get why you're here," I said. "With all the crap that happens on college campuses, it was stupid of me to joke about a gun."

"Do you own a gun?" the officer asked.

"I have a hunting rifle at my mom's house, but it's not here on campus," I explained.

The rifle was registered. They probably already knew I owned it.

"Do you own any other types of weapons?"

"Fuck you."

Yup.

I slowly shook my head. "No, sir."

"What about a dart gun?" the cop asked.

"A dart gun?" I laughed. "You're joking, right?"

"No joke. We found a disassembled dart gun in the dumpster," Tom said.

I shrugged. "Don't know what to tell you, Tom. It wasn't mine."

"Now, the electronics kit inside the apartment that looks like bomb parts, yeah, that's ours."

Shut up.

I scratched the back of my shaved head. "I wish I could help more."

Tom slowly nodded again like he was trying to convince himself of my truth.

"Listen, guys, if that's all, I'd *really* like to shower. My clothes are wet, I lost my best ski bag, and I'm hungry.

Poor Boy's was closed when I got there, and the union shut early." Two additional truths I slipped into the conversation.

"Yeah, sure." Tom nodded, and the campus cop followed suit.

They turned to leave, and I waited. I wasn't about to open my apartment door until they were gone. When they disappeared into the stairwell, I unlocked my door and darted inside.

Bonita was exactly where I'd left her. A length of rope was wrapped around her neck and tied to the water pipe in the apartment. When she looked up at me, her blue eyes no longer shone. They were kind of dull.

Neither Tom nor the cop would understand. They'd probably think it was a noose and that I was trying to hang her. It couldn't be further from the truth. I liked my cat. I was just fucking tired of cleaning up her messes.

CHAPTER 26

BRANSON

MY twin brother was the baseball player in the family, but I played Legion ball long enough to know the three-strike rule. Three strikes and you're out.

First strike: Professor Nigel caught me with the midterm exam. Strike two: missed the deadline for the scholarship essay he requested.

But seriously, what the hell?

Still, I was afraid of what strike three might look like. Lately my choices weren't hitting home runs. I was zero for two at bat.

When Nigel emailed that the window to send him the essay wasn't completely closed, I took the soft lob he threw. Writing an essay during midterm week—or anytime—wasn't what I wanted to do, but I wanted this monkey off my back more. I hated the feeling that I owed someone something.

I exhaled and set my cold IPA on the milk crate beside

the couch. My laptop was ready for something inspiring, but I had nothing. The only thing that inspired me was Hope. I wanted to drive back to Cheyenne and stare into her blue eyes. Instead, I stared at a black screen.

Describe a unique challenge you've undergone to pursue your education.

The essay's topic was as Hallmark as it got.

Fuck me.

I took a sip of the Harvest ale and texted Hope. **What's up?**

Rnt u supposed 2b wrtg an essay?

I laughed. **m/b**

M/b my ass. Listen, write da essay so we cn hang out nxt w/end n I cn beat u @ mario kart.

Ever since Hope checked out my Tinder profile, she'd been giving me shit. My pros and cons were legit. I knew how to start a fire with two sticks, I was a presentable plus one, and I did love camping and would take her with me. My cons were equally as real: I was not Ryan Reynolds, my baking skills would ruin anyone's diet, and I wouldn't let a girl beat me at Mario Kart. The last con got all the swipes—including Hope's. Now her whole mission was to kick my ass at the video game.

Nvr gonna happen, but cute idea, I replied.

We'll c. Get back2work talk 2night

I leaned against the couch. I didn't want to wait and talk to her later tonight; I wanted to talk to her now. But I also knew she was spending time with a family friend and couldn't talk. This family friend had already cut our weekend short, which sucked. I was back in Casper when I'd rather be in Cheyenne.

I sighed. The sooner I finished this bullshit, the closer I'd be to freedom from Nigel. I cracked my neck and started typing.

Branson Kovak
Scholarship Essay
Professor Nigel
Unique Challenge

During senior seminar this week, the topic of how we could better relate, understand, and support our community was discussed. The issue of schools and education was presented. We talked about the concerns and fears parents may have when first introducing their children into the classroom. Regardless of the community, the feelings that parents experience are similar.

A parent's job up until the first day of school is to be the sole protector of their child, but when they're introduced to their teacher, that changes. Now the teacher is the protector of this child. Parents have the right to be concerned. Growing up, I had many teachers, but none of them truly made me feel safe until fifth grade.

Throughout my childhood, I was faced with challenges that I would never wish on any kid my age. I was in constant fear in and outside of school from many different people in my young life.

There was a man in my life at home who constantly ruled the household with fear and paranoia that I had to witness along with the rest of my family. Then at school, I was clearly affected from the trauma. I stuttered and had a lisp. Even if I didn't speak, kids seemed to sense something was wrong, because I was constantly bullied and called a freak, or they wouldn't hang out with me at all.

I suffered this fate for many years until I was put in a testing situation with my fifth grade teacher, Mr. Brown. At this point in my life, whenever I was placed under tremendous stress, I would develop nervous ticks and my stuttering got worse. One day we were taking a standard quiz, which was nothing to be stressed about, but I began to do little coughs every couple of seconds. It was a sign of my tick. This occurred for several minutes until the teacher came over and put his hand on my shoulder.

He knelt next to me and whispered in my ear, "There is nothing to fear here. You are safe."

It wasn't until that moment that I realized I was cared for by someone outside of the terror I had been living with in my home. For the first time in my life, I felt completely and utterly safe somewhere.

I swallowed the emotions at the base of my throat and took a long drink. If my dad ever read this, he'd never speak to me again.

Don't quit now.

It wasn't Trevor or some command hallucination in my head, it was my own voice reminding me that I was more than my past. And at a base level, that internal voice reminded me that while my apartment might not be much, it was mine, and it was safe.

I've got this.

This time when my fingers touched the keys, they had purpose.

After that, I never had an issue while I was in class. I may not go on the path to become a teacher, but whatever path I do take, I want any child in my care to realize they're safe and that nothing bad will happen to them while they're with me.

If I were to be a teacher, I would utilize the same method and reassure all my students of their safety. There is nothing I won't do for someone who's hurting, because I understand what they've been through and have shed just as many tears as them.

Above anything else, a teacher should be a protector to students who can't protect themselves. We need more teachers like Mr. Brown. I believe there are some out there but not nearly enough.

I think as a working class, certain teachers become too focused on the end result of their job in regards to their own benefits rather than their students. Teachers are quite literally raising the next generation of adults, and this is a job that should never be taken lightly. I believe teachers should receive twice as many benefits and pay, because their job is the foundation for America and these children. If we underpay and underappreciate teachers, then they in return will underappreciate their students and jobs.

If we want to have any hope for a future, we need to take better care of the individuals living in that future. Teachers like Mr. Brown are so important to me because that one interaction changed my whole perspective on life and how I was living it. A life of constant fear and anxiety leads to very bad habits and traits. I am thankful that I never fully allowed those habits to take hold.

The unique challenges I had to pursue for my education began in my home and extended into the classroom until one teacher made me feel safe.

"Hell yes." I ran a spell check, attached it to an email to Professor Nigel, and hit Send. *Next stop, Cheyenne.* I knew Hope wasn't expecting me, but it wasn't like she'd get mad—especially since I planned on letting her win at Mario Kart.

CHAPTER 27

AARON

EVERYBODY these days liked to get things off their chest, so it was simply a matter of time before Hannah found out I'd hooked up with Amber during Halloween weekend. Maybe when my mom went to college, a person could do one thing at one school and not have the other school hear about it, but that was before Facebook, Instagram, and Snapchat. People posted pics, instant messaged, and took screenshots all in some vain effort to stay relevant. I wasn't a fan.

Hannah and I were in such a good place, and I didn't want it to end. I glanced out of my apartment window and saw her brown hair sticking out of her bike helmet like the tail of a kite trailing behind her. A guy could get lost in that hair. Or her goodness. Hannah was one of those genuinely good people who made me want to be a better person, even when it came to dealing with the morons on my volunteer house building team.

She parked her orange fat-tire cruiser that she called Archie and wrapped the bike chain through the frame and around the post.

I laughed and slid open the frosty window. "I think Archie's safe."

Hannah stomped her feet in the snow. "Stop." She giggled. "Archie's my only mode of transportation. If I lose him, I'm stuck. How would I get around campus?"

I shrugged. "There's always Lyft or Uber."

Her laughter increased. "Sure." She unsnapped her helmet and tossed her hair over her shoulder. "Don't I look like the kind of girl who would hire a driver?"

I mimicked her hair flip and shrugged. "High maintenance takes different shapes."

She removed her gloves and fanned them toward me. "You're crazy."

"No, that's my brother," I said, laughing at my own joke.

She shook her head before disappearing into the stairwell that led to my apartment. I opened the door just as she appeared on my doorstep.

"Hello." She leaned toward me, and I met her with a kiss. It was the kind of kiss that led to clothes coming off, which was what I hoped would happen.

She pressed against my chest, pushing me back. "We have to talk."

My stomach suddenly dropped like I was on a roller coaster. *Here it comes. She found out about Amber.*

"Okay." I led her toward the futon in my apartment, which functioned as both my bed and sofa.

She dropped her backpack on the floor beside her and sat on the edge like she wasn't sure she wanted to stay.

Why did I fuck this up?

"What's going on?" It felt like my heart jumped into my throat. It still beat just as fast and made it hard to swallow.

"I'm late."

I nodded. "For a midterm?"

When Hannah smiled, everything was right with the world. *Please don't leave me.*

"No." She shook her head. "Not a midterm. My period's late, and I'm never late."

Period. Late. It took a moment for what she'd said to sink in. "Pregnant?" I knew my voice changed, and I was pretty sure my face did as well. But not in a bad way, more in an oh-my-God kind of surprised way. "Are you pregnant?"

She reached into the front pocket of her backpack and withdrew a white-and-pink box. "I don't know. But we will in about—" She glanced at the side of the box. "—five to seven minutes."

I ran my palm over my head. "Wow. Okay." I jumped off the futon and reached for her. "Let's do this."

She took my hand but didn't move. "You're not mad?"

I squeezed her fingers. "Why would I be mad?"

"Aaron, I could be *pregnant*. We're in our senior year of college."

I smiled. "Yeah, you could be pregnant with *my* baby." I tilted my head and raised a single eyebrow. "It is *my* baby, right?"

Tears filled her eyes. "You're so crazy."

"No." I slowly shook my head. "That's my brother."

In seven minutes' time, I checked my email, made a cup of tea for Hannah, and continually stared at a pregnancy test for results that took six minutes to reveal.

"Is that…?" I asked beside her in the small bathroom of my apartment.

She turned toward me, tears streaming down her face.

"Okay," I said. "Okay. A baby. Wow. Okay, we got this." I didn't know who I was trying to reassure more.

Her crying intensified, and between sobs she said, "I can't do this. I have a plan. This isn't part of my plan."

Hannah needed more than reassurance. She needed something concrete. And I wasn't sure what that was.

She leaned her head on my shoulder, and I deeply inhaled. Today, she smelled like the sweet, rich fragrance of jasmine.

"Green apple with jasmine," she said between sniffles, as if reading my mind.

And that was when I knew we'd be okay. Hannah just got me. Other than Branson, no one understood me the way she did. So even though my head spun in a thousand different directions, I narrowed it down to one thought.

"When my mom first got sick," I shared about a topic I rarely, if ever, discussed, "I planted a jasmine tree outside her bedroom window in Casper. I wanted her to wake up or go to bed with the smell of jasmine. It's not too much or not enough but just the right amount." I kissed the top of

Hannah's head and held my lips there for a moment.

"What happened to the plant when you moved?" she asked, and I gently smiled.

Hannah was a native Clevelander. I was a Wyomingite.

"I uprooted it and brought it with me," I said.

Her eyes were red from crying, but they remained the most beautiful eyes I'd ever seen.

"Wyoming, huh?" she said like she was trying it on.

"Or Ohio." I wrapped my arm around her. "We've got nine months to figure it out."

"Aaron...."

"What?"

"I'm not sure I can do this."

What does that mean?

But I was too afraid to ask because I didn't want to know the answer. Instead, I held her against me and imagined the life we could have together.

CHAPTER 28

BRANSON

HOPE'S red car was parked along the street, and a black truck I didn't recognize was in her designated carport. I found a space a few spots ahead of her car.

I popped a mint into my mouth. The package promised three hours of fresh breath. If things went the way I planned, I'd only need it to last effectively for the first hour.

I tossed the mint tin on the passenger seat and stole a quick glance at myself in the rearview. Then Hope appeared in the frame. She was walking some guy out of her condo. Something stopped me from exiting my car. Instead, I watched from the rearview mirror.

She slipped her hand in his, then leaned up on her tiptoes, the way she did with me, and kissed him. It wasn't a peck on the cheek; it was an open-mouthed kiss on the lips. It was the kind of kiss she gave me before I left.

What? It felt like someone had sucker punched me. All the air left my lungs and sank to the pit of my stomach that was hollow with hurt.

Why would she do this to me?

He wrapped his arm around her waist and pulled her in to him. He was about my height, only fitter. He wasn't on meds that made him look like a melting marshmallow.

Who is he?

When he brushed her hair off her face and she smiled, my eyes stung.

Hope. I thought we were in love.

I loved her the way she loved on him. No matter how badly it hurt, I couldn't look away. The more I watched, the greater the divide grew between my heart and my head until I couldn't think straight.

I pushed open the door to my car and walked toward them. The dude saw me first. He took a measured step away from Hope, whose fair face grew fainter.

"Branson."

"Hey," I said inches away from them. Their body language shifted, no longer all cuddly and close. The guy started to flex his height against me when I shut that shit down.

"I'm Branson." I extended my hand to him.

"Jake." His handshake wasn't impressive.

"What are you doing here?" Hope's voice teetered on the edge of hysterical, and yet I found mine perfectly calm.

"Thought I'd surprise you," I said without looking at her. "Guess the joke's on me."

"Hey, I don't want any trouble." Jake held up his hands.

I slowly nodded. "No trouble. Just wanted to meet

Hope's *family friend*."

"Branson, it's not like that," Hope said, and I laughed.

"*Pretty* sure it is." I nodded toward her condo. "Could you just get my Mario Kart game?"

"But—"

"Yeah, it's not a parting gift. I need my game back."

She glanced at Jake and then back at me. Neither of us said anything. When it came to video games, bro code was strong.

Hope disappeared into her condo, and the silence between Jake and me got weird.

"I've actually got to get to work," he finally said.

I nodded. What was there to say? *Good luck fucking my girlfriend?* He walked toward his black truck, and Hope ran out of her condo toward him. That was when I knew. He was the one she wanted, not me.

When she reappeared, she practically threw the video game at me.

"Are you happy now?"

When I didn't respond, she continued to spiral.

"I told you I don't like to be alone," she said. "This shouldn't come as a surprise."

But it did. I thought we were in love. *I was. I was in love with you.* The words remained stuck somewhere between the Hope I'd had and the despair I now felt.

So I did the only thing I knew to do to stop from hurting.

I walked away.

CHAPTER 29

AARON

IN the twenty-four hours since I'd discovered my girlfriend was pregnant, I didn't think my feet hit the ground. What a feeling. I was going to be a dad. I wanted to spend every waking moment with Hannah, but she insisted that she fly solo for her appointment at the healthcare center on campus.

While I waited, I paced my apartment looking for something new to clean and continually checked my phone. No messages, emails, or missed calls. Every inch of my apartment was sanitized. *What's taking so long?*

I turned on my Bluetooth speaker that was linked to my phone. The Sheryl Crow version of "Here Comes the Sun" that was in *Bee Movie* played. Such a happy tune. Branson liked the Nina Simone cover, but I couldn't get into the jazz version—too damn depressing.

Carson always gave us shit that the original with her favorite Beatle was the best. I couldn't wait to tell my little sister that she was going to be an aunt. *She'll freak.*

I was so lost in my thoughts that I didn't hear her knock until I heard her call out, "Hey, let me in."

I opened the door, and a rush of cold air blew into the apartment. I gently pulled Hannah inside.

"Did you ride your bike? Is that okay to do? You know, with...."

The way her forehead wrinkled told me this was not a topic she wanted to discuss.

"Tea?" I asked, and she shook her head.

"Join me on the couch." She took my hand and led me to my futon that smelled like pine-scented cleaner. I didn't know how to clean a futon cushion, so I'd wiped it down with an antibacterial spray. Now I wished I hadn't.

"How'd things go?" My excitement was getting the best of me.

"I'm about five weeks pregnant," she said, and I couldn't help smiling, but she wasn't. "They checked my urine and then took blood."

"But you're pregnant, right?"

"Oh yeah, I'm pregnant."

"Okay that's good, right?" I gently squeezed her hand, which felt limp.

"Aaron, I've decided to terminate the pregnancy," she said, and just like when she told me she was late, it took a few seconds to register.

"Like an abortion?"

"Yes." Her voice never wavered. "I already made the appointment."

"What?" My raised voice did nothing to deter her.

"We live in Ohio."

"Yeah, and?"

"For a poli sci major, you sure are daft on local issues."

"Okay, I'm not sure how attacking me or my major will help clear this up for me." *What the fuck?*

"I'm sorry." Her hand no longer felt limp in mine, only cool to the touch. "The heartbeat law."

My mind blanked.

"It's against the law in Ohio to terminate a pregnancy after a fetal heartbeat is detected, which"—she squeezed my hand to stop my interruption—"is about five to six weeks into a pregnancy."

"Did they detect a heartbeat?"

She pulled away her hand. "No, Aaron, they didn't." She stood, and so did I.

"What? You come in here and lay this on me, and I'm just supposed to get on board with it?"

"Yeah, you are."

My eyes watered and my throat ached. I was still floating, but not in a good way. I felt myself tear apart—one part of me was in my apartment and another part of me watched everything that was happening from above.

"Can we talk about it?" I asked.

"Why? So you can try and change my mind?" She crossed her arms over her chest.

"No." I reached for her hand, but she kept it tucked against her.

"I don't need your consent," she said, which almost knocked me to my knees.

"Hannah." My voice pleaded with her for a different outcome.

Her eyes glistened with tears. "Aaron, please... please don't make this harder than it already is." She lowered her head. "I'm sorry."

I tried to keep it together, but all I could think of were the dreams I already had for us. "Can I go with you?"

When she looked up at me, her eyes told me her answer.

"Okay." I wanted to hold her, but she seemed too far away to reach. "Hey, why don't I make your favorite dinner— rice and chicken. We could binge-watch something. Maybe *Dead to Me*. I know you've wanted to see that."

A weak smile followed. "Not tonight. Maybe some other time?"

But we both knew there wouldn't be another time. When Hannah left, she'd never return. I would always be a reminder of something I was sure she'd want to forget.

There were so many things I wanted to say, but I didn't want anything to sound like pressure. That was the last thing I ever wanted to do to Hannah.

So I said what I thought she needed to hear, but it wasn't how I felt. It was so far from how I felt. "I'm so sorry this happened."

She wrapped her hands around her body like she was trying to hug herself, and it just about broke me.

"Oh, Hannah."

Tears streamed down her face. "I'll be okay."

But we wouldn't be okay. And I didn't know how to put us back together.

She kissed me on the cheek, and I bit the inside of my mouth to stop from losing it.

Then she turned toward the door, and I watched as she walked out of my life.

CHAPTER 30

DAVID AND ME

"**BONITA,** I'm back." I opened the closet where I'd left her with a bowl of water and food.

"Bonita?" I bent and gently touched her soft fur that was matted and cold. "Oh, Bonita. What happened?"

"She got what she deserved."

No one deserves this.

Her eyes were closed and her body was limp. "What have I done?"

Shame crept over me. *I'm too much like my dad.*

"Stop freaking out."

"Are you kidding me? She's dead. My cat's dead."

"It's a cat, not a child."

I rubbed my hand over my bald head. I still couldn't believe I'd shaved it. Everything was spiraling out of control.

"That's a little extreme. Your cat died. Big deal."

But it was. It was another loss. And the more that David

couldn't get that, the greater the distance between us grew.

"Bonita, I'm so sorry."

I went to the kitchen and grabbed the trash can and the broom. Bonita was heavier than I remembered. I carefully yet sturdily brushed her body into the garbage.

I didn't think it was possible to hurt more than I already did. My breakup stripped me raw.

I loved her. I thought she was the one. God, I really loved her.

"Love? You're joking, right?"

"Shut up. Shut up. Shut up."

"I'll be quiet once you get this shit out of your system. Fuck, just write about it. And now that the stupid cat's gone, you have no more excuses."

"Bonita wasn't stupid. If I hadn't listened to you, she'd still be alive."

"Bullshit. You hated her as much as I did. She took from you. She always took from you. Everyone takes from you."

I reached for the bottle on top of the refrigerator, broke the seal, and drank greedily. The sooner the amber-colored liquid got in me, the sooner everything would fade to black.

"Fuck this."

I couldn't agree more.

I opened my laptop and started typing, only this time I changed the title of my entry from "A Killer's Journal" to "A Killer's End."

A Killer's End

Every day I feel alone. My family has always been there for me, but my loneliness gets the better of me. I've always been betrayed by those who are closest to me, so I never fully feel committed to family or anyone who attempts to help me through life. Once I trust someone, it's only a matter of time before they stab me in the back. Or worse, break my heart.

Love is too heavy a price. It always brings sacrifice and despair. For all the love I've given, I've never truly received the benefits of its warmth. I've fought so hard to keep afloat in the darkness that always surrounds me, but every time I believe in the love of others, it only betrays me.

The only person you can depend on in this world is yourself. Once you lose sight of that, you're truly lost. Friends are an illusion. Even David. He's just another crutch so I don't have to face the grim reality that my life is meaningless. The only thing an individual can rely on is their own personal strength and how they do without someone. And the truth is I really don't have anyone.

The bottle of Wyoming whiskey beside me was a gift. And tonight it did exactly what I needed it to do.

I write so much better when I'm intoxicated because the fear of those reading my work disappears.

I normally write these entries when I'm drunk. It allows me to release feelings that are usually too much for me to handle when I'm sober.

Relationships die all the time. So do people. Why should I ever feel bad about either? There were so many times throughout my childhood where I wished my father would die, yet for some reason, God ignored my prayers and focused on someone less important.

David may be the name of the voice in my head, but he is ever so real and takes control whenever I choose to lose control, especially when drinking. He's promised to never bring harm to me, my twin brother, or anyone in my family, but Bonita is dead, so his word is worthless. It also needs to be known that when I disappear, that's when things get bad. And right now things are really bad.

Emotions and love work well for most people but not me. No sooner do I begin to feel the warmth of love and think that maybe things will work out for me than love betrays me.

All I want is for someone to love me—I mean truly love me—the way I love them. I want someone who will make sense of David. He's only as strong as he is because no one is stronger. There is no one who protects me the way he does. And he never leaves. Everyone I've loved leaves.

I paused for a moment, stretching my fingers.

"See, writing helps. I'm the only one who stays. Everyone else leaves."

"Not everyone leaves." I shut my laptop and picked up my phone. There was one person who hadn't left me—yet.

She picked up on the first ring.

"Mom."

"Aaron, what's wrong?"

CHAPTER 31

DAVID AND AARON

I didn't know how she knew that I needed her. I lowered my head, and the years of hiding rolled down my face.

"Sweetheart, are you okay? What's going on?"

"I'm…." I didn't know where to begin.

"*Now what? Are you* really *going to tell her about* all *the things you've done? How about that sorority girl duct-taped to the goalpost? Why not start there? That's a good ice breaker.*"

You did that!

"*Sure, keep telling yourself that lie.*"

I didn't know what you did until after *it happened. And even then I wasn't sure.*

"*Oh, buddy, that's what every psycho says.*"

I didn't! You took over my thoughts. I was lost to your influence.

"*Do you even hear yourself? You sound weak and pathetic, and we both know your mom doesn't do either of those well."*

You're wrong. She's my mom. She'll understand. I'm her son.

"No, Branson's her son. You're just the spare."

"Aaron, please, you're scaring me. Say something."

"My cat died."

"Oh." She took a beat. "I'm sorry." A moment passed. "I didn't know you had a cat. Does your apartment complex and lease allow that?"

"Lease? She's more concerned with how this will affect her deposit. She doesn't care about you."

Shut up.

"Sweetie?"

"If this was Branson, she'd already be in the car driving to him."

The more David and my mom competed to be heard, the more I sank into the darkness. It felt like I was drowning, and I just needed someone to throw me a lifeline. I reached for the bottle and drank until I thought I'd puke.

"What can I do?" she asked.

Grab it. My voice, not David's. I wiped my mouth on the sleeve of my shirt. *Tell her.*

"Ma, I'm not okay." My voice cracked, and I began crying. "My cat died, my girlfriend's pregnant but she's not keeping it, and I'm pretty sure I'm losing my mind."

"Oh, Aaron." Her voice was home. "Pregnant? Oh, sweetheart."

I swallowed, but my voice was still stuck in my throat.

"That's *a lot.* You're not losing your mind," she said

with a gentle chuckle. "Dear Lord, that's a lot for anyone."

I nodded. "Yeah it is."

"That's right. Keep it to the minor league. Cat died, girlfriend's pregnant—she can handle that."

Fuck you.

"So tell me about this girlfriend," she said.

"We're not together anymore."

"I'm sorry. Is she okay?"

"If you mean did she have the abortion yet, I don't know," I said and instantly regretted it.

"That's not what I meant."

"Ma, I'm sorry. It freaks me out how much I'm like Dad."

"Don't say that. You're *nothing* like your father," she insisted.

"No, seriously I am. I would get super angry at my cat and hit her." I tested the waters. How much could I tell my mom?

"Is that how she died?"

It was a legitimate question, but it made me sick. I took another chug before I answered.

"No. I mean, I don't think that's what killed her. I'd get these heat flashes and hit her with the broom or a dart gun." Every crime against my cat poured forth as easily as the whiskey. "She was always making a mess, so I tied her to the water heater."

My confession was met by silence.

"Ma?"

"I'm listening," she said, and I laughed.

"Or are you trying to figure out how to disown me?" I asked.

"Aaron." Her tone was sharp. "I'm trying to understand. The things you're telling me don't sound like you. That's not my son."

"Ma, you don't know what I'm capable of."

"I'm sure that's true. But I know *you*." Her voice cracked. "I know my son. And he's the light of my life."

I lowered my head. "No, Ma, that's Branson. Or Jack. It's not me."

"Is that what you think?"

I shrugged. "Ma, I'm the one you go to when things are broken."

There was a brief pause, like she was weighing what I'd said against the truth. "Oh God, Aaron, I'm sorry. That was never my intention."

"Eh, it's nothing." I tried to brush it aside the way I did with Bonita. "I'm used to it."

"Sweetheart, I think you've had a lot going on, and it sounds like you may need to talk to someone."

I laughed. "Jesus fucking Christ, Ma. I just told you that I tied my cat to a water heater and occasionally hit her, that my girlfriend would rather terminate our baby than have a relationship with me, and you think I may need to talk to someone? I think that ship sailed a long time ago—like when I was five and you hid me in the washing machine so Dad wouldn't find me. Remember that? Or how about the many times you got that babysitter who locked us in the closet so he could have his buddies come over. Maybe if

I talked to someone back then, I wouldn't be so fucked up now."

The only sound I heard was the muffled cries of my mother.

"Oh, Aaron, I'm so sorry."

"Don't do that. Don't apologize for what Dad did."

"You'll find out when you get older that when your children are hurt, you hurt."

"Yeah, Mom, I kind of get that. I have a child—"

"You had a child."

Fuck you, David.

"Are you ready for a baby?" she asked.

The question took me off guard. It was like my mind blanked before I could answer. "I don't know."

"A baby is a full-time responsibility. It's a lot for anyone. I was in my late twenties when I had you and your brother, and I wasn't nearly prepared."

"That's because of Dad."

"No." Her response was instant. "There were a lot of good years between your father and I before… before the abuse progressed."

My mom didn't talk about her marriage to my dad. Or not with me, at least. I didn't get the heartfelt talks; I got the to-do lists. I sank into my futon, tucked my bottle beside me, and listened.

"It's taken me *years* of counseling to understand the control dynamic that was in my relationship with your father. It was there from the get-go, but I was young and in love and only saw what I wanted to see," she said.

I did the same thing with Hannah.

"But even with your dad by my side, I was overwhelmed by the thought of motherhood. I didn't know if I had what it took." She softly laughed. "And I'm sure you and your brother would agree I was in over my head. I know I wasn't ready for a baby when I was in college." She paused. "Anyway, I'm not sure if any of this helps you."

Her voice felt like a hug.

"Hannah said it wasn't part of her plan."

"That must've been hard for her to tell you. And I'm sure it wasn't easy for you to hear."

"Yeah, she was pretty broken up."

"I imagine. Aaron, I don't know any woman who makes that decision lightly. I know I didn't."

I sat up and the bottle rolled away from me. "What? *You* had an abortion?"

"I did."

"When? Was it with dad?"

"Oh, Lord, no. He was too controlling with sex. There wasn't any chance for an accidental pregnancy."

"Okay, ew."

She laughed. "Well, you did ask."

"So if it wasn't with Dad, then when did it happen? Was it with Jack's father?" I never mentioned that scumbag's name. I didn't know what was worse, an abusive father or one who abandoned his child. My little brother was only four when that douchebag hitched up his fifth wheel to his truck and walked out on us. He left my mom and his only son so he could be with his "one true soul mate." Turned out his soul mate was Megan, a much younger woman he used to work with at some cattle ranch. *Whatever. I hope he got a disease.*

"Why are you focusing on him? Some people are just damaged goods."

I shook my head, trying to ward off David's voice. *Shut up.*

"No, it wasn't with Jeff. It happened much earlier in my life. Right after college," she said, and my mind was blown.

"Really? Who was the guy? What'd he think?"

"I don't know."

"What do you mean? You don't know who the father was?"

She laughed. "No, I know who the father was, but I never told him."

Her honesty pushed me back into the futon. "Mom, that's pretty fucked up. He had a right to know."

"That *may* be where we differ."

"What the hell, Mom? It was his child too."

"Aaron, there were circumstances.'"

"What does that mean?"

"It means that it's something I don't talk about and won't discuss with my son. But I can tell you that it was one of the hardest decisions I've ever made."

"Do you regret it?"

"No." Her voice regained strength. "I think that's why I don't dwell on it. At the time, it was the right decision and the choice that made the most sense with where I was in my life."

"Huh."

"But this isn't about me," she said. "You've lost your cat and now this young woman."

"Hannah. Her name's Hannah."

"Aaron, it's a lot. Plus, you're in your senior year of college. There's a lot on your plate."

"Yeah, maybe it's better this way. It's not like I can change anything."

"Couldn't you?"

Shut up.

"Sweetheart, if cancer has taught me anything, it's to not dwell on the things you can't change. I can't change that I had cancer—or have. But I can change how I view it. You can't change that your cat died. And you can't change what happened with you and this young woman. All you can control is what *you* can change."

When I didn't say anything, she continued.

"You can change how you treat animals. And you can change how you view this breakup. You can focus on it and hurt and shut yourself off from the world, and trust me when I say I know *that* doesn't work. *Or* you can choose to move on."

"It's not that easy," I said.

"Oh, dear heavens, don't I know that. It's not easy, and it stinks. There's a time to mourn, because that's what it boils down to is loss. When I lost parts of my body, I had to mourn that. So feel the hurt, but just don't get stuck in it."

I nodded as if she could see the gesture.

"I'm not sure if Branson's told you, but he started

going to this counseling center on campus. It has an awful name like 'depression depot' or something like that. I can't remember, but I know it's helping him. Is there something like that at your campus?"

"I don't know." And I didn't. "Ma, I'm not a fan of shrinks. I mean, look at what happened with Branson. He's had two different shrinks, and they always screw with his medications. And Trevor *still* came back. It was a nightmare."

"This isn't a psychiatrist, it's a therapist."

"Yeah, well, I'm not *that* far gone. I have things under control. Branson's problem is that he lost control and let Trevor take over."

"Trevor came back because Branson didn't know what was happening to him."

"Oh, he knew. Trust me, Mom, *he knew.* It's hard not to know."

"Aaron." Her voice subtly shifted. "What do you mean?"

I shook my head. "Nothing."

"No, it's not nothing. Are you hearing voices?"

"Look at Mom. Isn't that the million-dollar question? So now what?"

I don't know. Shut up.

"Is that why you thought you were losing your mind?" Her tone was filled with tension. "Do you need to see a psychiatrist?"

"I don't know what I need, Mom. But I don't need a lecture."

"This isn't lecturing, Aaron." Her backbone came out

when I sounded like my dad, who forever told her she lectured him. "I'm your mom, and I'm worried. You're an identical twin. There's something like a *40* percent chance that you could have schizoaffective disorder."

"Not that you did the research," I said.

"Of course I did the research. I'd be a fool not to."

"I don't like this version of your mom."

It was the first time in a while that David and I agreed.

"Yeah, well, I've done my own research. I know about the genetic predisposition, but that's all it is. There's no evidence that says I'll be as screwed up as my brother."

"Stop! That's enough. Your brother is no more responsible for his mental illness than a diabetic is responsible for their diabetes."

"Oh, but that *may* be where we differ," I said, mimicking her. "Someone can eat their way into diabetes the same way your favorite son fanned the flame of his psychosis. The first time he had a mental break, I get it, he didn't know. But when Trevor came back, he knew. But hey"—I shrugged—"it was Branson, so no one held him accountable."

"That's not true."

"Shit, sell that to someone who'll buy it, like Carson or Jack. They're still drinking your Kool-Aid."

"Aaron."

"Uh-oh. Now you did it."

Shut up. You're not helping.

"Oh, what, Mom, too harsh?" The alcohol finally did what I wanted—I no longer felt anything. I was numb.

"Think about it," I said. "Branson's always been different.

He never lived up to Dad's expectations, and he's never gotten past that. And Dad did him no favors. Dad was tough on him, but *you* were too soft. And I was left in the middle of your chaos to make everything okay. Branson *never* had a good balance, but don't for a second think that he didn't know about his mental illness."

"*Shit.*"

Shut up.

"He knew. There's no way *not* to know. It's a little hard to ignore the voices, *Mom.* Branson knew about Trevor the same way I knew about David. The difference is I know how to keep that shit in check. Your sweet Branson is too soft for that. And for the record, he's *not* a diabetic, so stop using that as your excuse. It's messed up. Branson's mental. He *chose* to let that psychopath Trevor run his life and ruin ours."

"Where are you?" Her tone was way too maternal, like I was in trouble or something.

"What?"

"Aaron, where are you?"

"I'm in my apartment." *What the fuck?*

"She's going to lock you up just like she did to Branson."

She wouldn't do that. She loves me.

"I need you to stay there," she said.

"Why?"

"Aaron, promise me you won't leave."

She's going to send me away.

The darkness descended upon me, and I began to sink into its inky depths.

"Aaron, I need you to stay where you are until I can get there."

David cut the air with my hand. "Yeah, don't think that's going to happen, Tara."

CHAPTER 32

BRANSON

I walked across the commons toward my car that was parked on the ass-end of campus. A banner stretched across two buildings announcing the winter Mozart music festival.

Hope loved classical music.

The banner buoyed back and forth against Wyoming's wind. If I could reach up and yank it down, I would. I knew the music nerds in my English Lit class thought the music festival was the end-all—but it wasn't.

Know what's cool? Not celebrating a seventeenth-century composer.

The sky was dark and it wasn't even noon. Ever since Hope and I broke up, it seemed like the world had turned gray. The semester was finally wrapping up, but I was just going through the motions. At this point, I didn't even need to go to my classes to pass.

What am I doing here?

I grabbed my phone. There was a missed call from my

mom but no voice mail. I'd learned that with cancer, no news was good news. I speed-dialed Aaron. The call went directly to voice mail. After I left him a message, I scrolled to the airline app, but the farther I walked away from the commons, the slower it loaded. I stopped moving and waited beside the humanities building for the flights out of Casper to Cleveland to appear on the screen. No surprise that there weren't any direct flights, but if I got to the airport by two, I could be in Cleveland by seven their time.

I purchased the ticket, saved it to the app, and smiled. I couldn't wait to see the look on Aaron's face when I showed up on his doorstep.

CHAPTER 33

DAVID AND AARON

I flipped up my laptop screen and began typing.

A Killer's End

I know how this has to end. It won't be fun, but living between sanity and insanity ain't no picnic. I've done things I never thought I was capable of doing, and I'm hurting more people. I hurt my mom, the one person who's off-limits. I hurt her. Worse, I scared her. She must be losing her mind right now. I have no choice but to end things. The longer I let David be part of me, the more hurt I'll inflict.

I. Am. Done.

I stared at the journal entry.

"I don't hurt you."
"Yeah, sure, and Santa Claus is real."
"We're both as real as you need us to be."

The sooner I got him out of my head, the better.
I continued to write.

There's no pill big enough to choke him. David's been with me since I was five, or at least that's my earliest recollection of him. He was there with me in the dark, locked closet when Branson wet himself and I had to be the big brother, the protector. David was mine. But he's not protecting me anymore. I'm a ticking time bomb here.

A part of me is afraid that I have the same shit Branson has. It's terrifying.

David broke through. *"What's terrifying about it?"*
"Everything. I mean, seeing Branson have his moments, his breaks. Not fun."
The only way to ignore David was to write.

I've tried so hard not to be like Branson. Seeing my brother in that hospital and the lack of control he had over his life was fucked up. His inability to have control over his thoughts was scary. Then the hospital cut him off from the real world. He didn't have access to basic shit, like a cell phone. I think that scared the shit outta me more than anything. It was like they kept him hostage. The hospital decides who's freed and who remains locked up. Fuck that.

I can't be like him. It's why I don't do street drugs. I don't want something to trigger a psychotic break. That's what they called it when it happened to Branson, a psychotic break.

All the people who stayed in the hospital were a mess. One day this one girl died like right after I got there. I walked past her room and she was pearl white. It wasn't like anything I'd ever seen. She was like one of those glass China dolls that Carson used to collect. It was freaky as fuck. I wasn't even thinking about death or that Branson could die from this. I went into his room and we just bawled our eyes out.

My cell rang with an incoming call. Branson. I let it go straight into voice mail.

"Your mom isn't coming for you. She sent Branson."

"Fuck you." I shook my head. "You don't know that. It could be one of those twin things, like when we were in high school and I knew something was wrong, so I called him and his girlfriend told me he had fallen off his moped and skinned up his side real badly. It's a twin thing. That's all it is."

His laughter mocked me.

"Your mom will never come for you. You may be the firstborn twin, but you're not her first priority."

I hate you.

My phone chimed with a text from the seller I'd contacted. He had the gun I needed, and since it was a private sale, there was no background check required. There were so many loopholes in gun laws that my little brother, Jack, could walk into a pawn shop, and if they weren't a licensed dealer, he could walk away with a gun. Okay, maybe not a gun. But if he was twenty-one he could.

The thought of my little brother put a lump in my throat.

He'll be better off. It's better to feel pain than to have others endure it.

I refocused my attention to the text and responded that our meeting in two hours was still on. This time I wouldn't draw attention to myself. I grabbed my backpack and left my apartment like it was any other school day.

CHAPTER 34

BRANSON

"**HEY,** Mom, what's up?" I balanced my cell against my ear and shoulder while I unloaded my pockets and stepped out of my shoes. My keys, loose change, and wallet went in a tub on the conveyor belt.

"Sir, *all* electronics need to go through." The TSA agent was a woman about my mom's age.

"Mom, I'll call you right back." Before she could respond, I ended the call and tossed my phone in a circular bin that slowly moved toward the X-ray machine.

Casper's airport was small, which was great for last-minute travel. It was less than ten minutes from my apartment with free parking, so other than stuffing jeans, a couple shirts, and other stuff into a bag, leaving Wyoming didn't take much effort.

I wasn't stupid enough to think that Ohio would fix my shattered heart, but it'd be a start.

Passing through TSA and getting to the gate took just

over five minutes. Wyoming wasn't for everyone, but it was for me. Aaron seemed to think I wanted to leave Wyoming and put it in my rearview, but I'd never leave. My dream job was to work at one of the state parks and call the outdoors my office. I was one semester away from that happening. Dr. Blaze's whole spiel about focusing on the positive wasn't for nothing.

I wasn't looking forward to my next appointment with him, though. There was no way to spin that into something other than what it was. I was not ready to see Hope again.

Maybe she'll quit.

Sure, and maybe pigs'll fly.

The hurt was too fresh. No matter how many times I tried to think of what I could've done differently, there was a part of me that knew there was nothing.

I dropped my bag on a blue seat in the boarding area and called my mom.

"Sorry about that," I said when she picked up.

"Is this a good time? Do you have a minute?"

I glanced at the clock on the wall. "Yeah, my plane doesn't take off for another twenty minutes. What's up?"

"Plane? Where are you?"

I laughed. "Uh, Casper, where I live. I'm at the airport." I stood in front of the wall of glass and watched the planes on the tarmac. "I'm going to see Aaron, but don't tell him. I want it to be a surprise. You know, like when he flew home to see you."

"Oh, okay."

The drop in her voice wasn't what I expected.

"Don't you think it's a good idea?"

"No, it's not that. I'm worried about your brother," she said. "I spoke to him, and he's not himself. And now he won't answer my calls."

"Mom, it's the end of the semester. *No one* is themselves. He's probably studying. It's just the time of year."

"No, that's not it. I think Aaron is having a mental breakdown."

"What?" I shook my head. "Mom, Aaron is the strongest person I know. He's probably just stressed, that's all. You know Aaron, he freaks if he doesn't get a 4.0."

"I don't think that's it. He talked about Trevor and how you had to have known about the voices, and then he mentioned someone named David. Does he have any friends named David?"

"Not that I know about." A plane landed in the distance. I glanced at the clock. My flight would be boarding in less than twenty minutes. "Mom, what exactly did Aaron say?"

"He talked about Trevor and how you would've known he was back and that it's hard not to know about the voices. That's when he mentioned David and said you just know."

"Know what?"

"The voices. That if you have them, you know."

If I hadn't called my mom, I would've thought this was some prank. *What the fuck?*

"Did he actually say that? Did he say he was hearing voices?"

"No, he didn't come out and say it, but after…."

"It's okay, Mom, I'm not going to break. Just say it.

After me, you're worried."

"Branson, I'm *really* worried. I can't fly out there until my oncologist gives me the go-ahead, but I don't think I can wait."

"Okay, well, I'm headed there now."

"What if it's too late?"

The last time I heard my mom this scared was when I was in the hospital.

"I called the university, and they put me in touch with the campus patrol, who promised they'd do a welfare check on him. But that was hours ago, and they haven't called back. Branson"—her voice cracked—"what if he's not okay?" She started crying, and my eyes welled.

"Mom, he's going to be okay. It's Aaron. He has to be okay."

Her crying intensified. "I missed it. Branson, I missed it. He came home and needed me, and I wasn't there for him. How did I miss this?"

"Mom, you've got to stop. We don't know anything." The door to the plane opened and a flight of stairs descended. "Listen, they're going to start boarding the plane."

"He broke up with his girlfriend and she's pregnant," she blurted out.

"Hannah? Hannah's pregnant."

A flight attendant appeared behind the kiosk and picked up the mic.

My mom began to talk, but I couldn't hear her over the PA.

"Good afternoon. This is the preboarding announcement

for flight 86 to Denver. We are now inviting those passengers with small children and any passengers requiring special assistance to begin boarding at this time."

It was the middle of the week. There weren't any children or elderly people flying to Denver.

"Regular boarding will begin in approximately five minutes. Thank you."

"What'd you say?"

"I'm sorry," she said in a voice that could only be described as resigned.

"Mom, it's going to be okay, I promise. This is Aaron we're talking about. He's probably just feeling *really* down because of Hannah. Breakups suck." I thought of my own, which suddenly seemed stupid.

Hannah's pregnant? Fuck.

"Did Aaron say what they're going to do?"

"She's chosen not to have the baby" was all my mom would say on the topic.

"Oh."

The flight attendant spoke again. "This is the boarding call for passengers booked on flight 86 to Denver."

"Mom, I've got to get on the plane."

"Be safe."

I laughed. "Mom, it's Aaron. The worst thing he could do to me is cook for me."

That made her laugh. "I can't think of a better time for you to be there for him. Please call me. As soon as you're with your brother, call me. When I hear from my doctor, I'll be there."

"I've got this."

"But I'm his mom." Her voice broke again.

"Aaron knows that. He knows you'd be there if you could."

"No, I *will* be there. I will be there for my son."

"Mom, it's going to be okay. But I've got to get on the plane."

"I love you. Call me." I knew if she could stay on the phone until I got to Cleveland, she would. There was nothing my mom wouldn't do for her kids.

"I'll call. Love you, Mom."

CHAPTER 35

BRANSON

FROM the moment my mom mentioned David, I scrolled through all of Aaron's social media accounts. There wasn't one David anywhere on any of his feeds. Still I continued to check. Friends of Aaron's, friends of Hannah—anyone connected to my brother, I checked. And I continued to come up empty.

Who's David? Is he my brother's version of Trevor? Could that be possible?

The flight from Casper to Denver was a blur, as was the connecting flight from Denver to Cleveland. When the captain made the announcement that we'd be landing soon, I glanced out my window and caught the sun above a floor of clouds as it began to set. I snapped a quick pic. From this height, everything seemed manageable.

A "Welcome To Cleveland" sign greeted me in the

airport, which was deceptively bigger than it appeared. I followed the other passengers toward baggage claim. Other than our group, the airport was virtually empty, and it was only seven. I turned at a navy-painted wall that had "Cleveland" plastered in white and took the stairs toward the front entrance.

Even though it was November, the moisture in the air made it feel colder than Wyoming. The exterior of the airport was under construction. The plywood sheets covering the worksite were painted with scenes from the city of Cleveland. An image of Superman with his hands proudly on his hips announced that Cleveland was the birthplace of the action hero.

When we were little, anytime Aaron and I pretended to be superheroes, he chose Superman. I was always Batman.

My eyes watered and I swallowed hard.

He's fine.

I scanned the license plates of the cars lined up outside the airport until I found the Lyft I'd ordered. Aaron's address was already logged as my final destination. The app claimed I'd be at my brother's apartment in fifteen minutes.

With all the city lights, the sky looked like a bruised plum. The city blurred past me in a stream of colors. When the driver pulled into the apartment complex, I did a double take. A tall, elongated, tan-colored brick building loomed ahead. It was almost a duplicate of our freshman dorm at Nickel Hall. That beast was a twelve-story building with great views that overlooked the campus and an elevator that never worked. Aaron and I were on the eighth floor, which absolutely sucked.

Aaron was on the seventh floor in this building. I walked past an empty pool on the way to a side entrance. I didn't want to announce myself, which would've been the only way to enter the locked building. But four years of apartment life told me that a side door would be propped open by a rock or, in this case, a sneaker. The freight elevator was off to the side of the main elevator. I slung my bag over my shoulder, pressed the button for the seventh floor, and for the first time in a long time, I prayed.

"Hey, it's me. I know I don't do this until I need something, but…." I swallowed. *"This isn't for me; it's for my brother. He's always been there for me and now…."* I shook my head. *"I don't know who this David is. God, please just keep him safe. Let him be okay."*

CHAPTER 36

AARON

"YOU'RE *not going to do it.*"

The louder David became, the more determined I had to be, but it was getting harder and harder to shut him out.

The handgun was smaller than I'd expected, but it'd do the trick. I only needed one shot.

I opened the laptop and created a new document.

My lip trembled and my hands shook.

"See, you don't have the stomach for this."

I wiped my eyes against the sleeve of my shirt. Fuck, David was right. I didn't have the stomach for this. I didn't even know how to write the letter.

"If you're determined to do this, let me write the letter."

You'll talk me out of it.

"Nah, it's probably one of your better plans."

Be nice.

"Always."

This time when I wrote, I let David speak through me.

Mom,

I'm sorry. You don't deserve this. I hope that someday you'll forgive me. My entire life I've wanted to make you proud. And the truth is I've done things you'd never understand and couldn't possibly forgive. Even if you did, things would change between us. I don't want you to ever look at me differently. But I know that when you discover what David and I did, you'd never look at me the same way again. I don't even remember some of the stuff, only that I know we did stuff that wasn't right.

My hands shook and tears flooded down my face. *I can't do this.*

"That's because you're not supposed to. Let me do it for you."

I nodded. There was an odd sense of peace knowing David would handle it.

"Let's finish the letter."

Mom, you'll want to think it's your fault, but it's not. In the genetic gene pool, Branson and I got dealt a bad hand. And the best way to play a bad hand is to do the one thing no one ever expects—fold.

Folding is final. It takes you out of the game, but sometimes conceding that you've lost is the hardest, most honest truth to face. I haven't been living with the truth for such a long time; it actually feels good to know that it's still somewhere inside me.

The other thing that no one ever thinks about is that when you fold, it allows the other player a better chance. And there's no one who deserves a win more than Branson. He's lived in my shadow and then Trevor's. I was always the more popular twin, which was all Branson ever wanted. He just wanted to fit in, and I was too much of a dick to give him that. When I'm gone, he can finally have it. Branson means everything to me, and he's been through enough. It's time he gets the win.

I love you, Mom.

I printed the letter and placed it with the other documents that were on top of my laptop, wanting everything to be easily found. I carefully arranged my keys, wallet, and cell phone neatly beside the computer, then picked up the gun and went to the futon, the place where my life started crumbling.

I'd just closed my eyes and imagined how everything would end when someone suddenly knocked on my door.

CHAPTER 37

BRANSON

WHEN Aaron opened the door, I almost didn't recognize him. His head was shaved, his eyes were sunken, and he was super skinny. He looked like a deranged skinhead zombie. He held a gun against his thigh as if I wouldn't see it. As soon as he spoke, I knew someone else was doing all the talking.

"Leave and shut the fucking door behind you."

"Aaron, I can't do that." I slowly took a step inside his apartment.

"Listen, fucktard, one more move and I'll blow your brains out."

"Just let me take a piss. I've been on a plane all afternoon, and you know I've got the bladder of a little girl," I said.

The shift seemed to startle him. He nodded toward the bathroom, which was down the hall from his living room.

"Make it fast."

"Yup." I glanced at the apartment, which was in move-in or more like move-out condition. The walls were barren and looked like they had been wiped clean, the carpet had fresh vacuum marks, and a strong scent of pine filled the air. I purposefully walked past his desk and caught a glimpse of the papers on his laptop. I skimmed the first line, and suddenly I couldn't breathe.

"Aaron...." I didn't care that he had me locked in his sights.

He turned and reached for my arm, but I grabbed the printed pages before he could.

A Killer's End

I know how this has to end.

I flipped to the page behind it.

Mom,

I'm sorry. You don't deserve this. I hope that someday you'll forgive me. My entire life I've wanted to make you proud. And the truth is I've done things you'd never understand and couldn't possibly forgive. Even if you did, things would change between us. I don't want you to ever look at me differently. But I know that when you discover what David and I did, you'd never look at me the same way again. I don't even remember some of the stuff, only that I know we did stuff that wasn't right.

David. He was real to my brother, and that made him all the more dangerous. The thing about having auditory hallucinations was that it made it really hard to focus. These voices—or in mine and my brother's cases, the singular voice—grow so loud it makes it almost impossible to concentrate on anything other than what that voice says. Sometimes the auditory hallucination whispers, other times it comforts, but the worst is when it becomes aggressive. It made connecting with the outside world almost impossible. Having someone talk in my head completely isolated me from everyone around me. Instead of talking to others, the impulse was to talk back to the voice. Dealing with that voice on a day-to-day basis caused me to become really depressed. It was a side effect of the constant criticism. And left untreated, the voice became so dominant, it commanded me to do things I normally wouldn't. The gun in my brother's hand and his suicide note were proof that David's voice had drowned out Aaron's ability to hear or connect to anyone else—even me.

Everything I knew about surviving this mental illness crumbled inside. It was a battle I wouldn't wish on anyone, least of all my best friend and twin. Tears streamed down my face faster than I could wipe them away.

"Aaron." I clutched the papers in my hand and turned to

the brother who was beside me my whole life. "This isn't the answer."

"It's the only way to make it stop."

For a second, I heard my brother and saw him behind eyes I didn't recognize.

"We can figure this out. We always have. It's always been us. We've seen our way through tougher shit." I threw the papers toward the desk.

In response, he tapped his chin with the barrel of the gun, which was when I realized just how strong David was in his ear.

"Don't let him win," I said. "Jesus, Aaron, don't let that bastard get the best of you. He's playing you. He's making you think this is your idea when it's all his. You're stronger than him."

A sinister smile crossed his face.

"It's cute that you think Aaron is strong."

Fucker. David was toying with us.

So I toyed right back.

"Listen." I purposefully sidestepped referring to Aaron's command hallucination by any name. The more impersonal I could make him, the less control he had. "I get that you *think* you know Aaron, but you don't. I do. You only know a *part* of him. But I know *everything* about him."

When David remained silent, I continued.

"For starters, I know my brother sleeps best on his side with a pillow bunched up against him. He says he holds it like a football when he actually holds it the way he used to hold his stuffed Bert. He was Bert and I was Ernie. And together we were unstoppable."

Nothing seemed to register a reaction, so I went for broke.

"Do you like me, Bert?" I held my breath and waited. Whenever things got tense between us, I tossed out that line and it was like a magic salve. It always worked.

But he said nothing.

I slowly nodded and delved right back in. "I also know that my brother's favorite hangover food is a five-dollar box from Taco Bell and that when he's scared, he sings to himself. But not just any song. My big brother sings that damn Barney song that's annoying as fuck, but it's what he sings when he's bugging out."

He placed the gun toward his temple. I wiped my nose in the crook of my arm and tried to blink away the tears that blurred my vision. David could not have my brother.

"Goddamn it! Aaron, I know you hear me. I know you're still in there." I wanted to grab him by the shoulders and shake him, but I was afraid David would pull the trigger, and I wasn't sure who he'd kill first.

"Do you remember what you did when Trevor returned—hell, I don't know if he ever left—but when you realized Trevor was still fucking with me, do you remember what you did?"

I crossed my arms over my chest to stop from shaking. I was scared and mad, and I didn't know what I was doing. All I knew was I was in a standoff between him and David. And I wasn't going to leave until my brother returned. I wouldn't leave until I saw Aaron's face, not the hollowed, empty expression that wasn't him.

"What you shared with Aaron is the past." He lowered the gun from his temple. "It doesn't matter now." His voice had an edge that was undeniable. I'd hit a nerve, and Aaron's command hallucination didn't like it.

"It *does* matter. It matters to me and to Aaron and, hell, to our whole fucked-up family. It's always been Aaron and me. It matters."

But nothing registered. I was talking about externals when I needed to go internal.

"You saved *my* life. You told me I was worth saving. Aaron, I know you hear me." I bridged the distance between us, and David's hold on the gun tightened until his knuckles looked white.

"Do you remember how you told me that I *wasn't* like dad and that Trevor *wasn't* my voice? Do you remember that? Because I do. You told me Trevor was nothing more than a voice and that he *wasn't* part of me, that he just coped for me when I couldn't. But what saved me wasn't all those great things you said but what you did."

All those emotions—shame, regret, sorrow—from that dark time in my life rose to the surface. And as much as I wanted to push them back down, that wouldn't help my brother. I stood before him and let my soul speak.

"When I got out of the hospital the second time, everyone wanted me to be okay, but I wasn't, and the only person who got that was you. *You knew.* You knew I still wasn't a hundred percent, so you gave up your college plans for me. You gave up everything." My voice trembled.

"Aaron, when you stayed and went to college with me to make sure Trevor was gone for good, you believed in my recovery when everyone around me had their doubts. Then you stayed sophomore year just to make sure Trevor never came back. And he didn't. He's gone, Aaron, and that's *all* because of you."

The truth settled in my body like a peace I'd never known. Aaron saved me, and I was the only one who could save my brother.

In a move that startled us both, I grabbed Aaron's wrist and instinctively pivoted away from the barrel. But I couldn't break his grip on the gun, and I wasn't thinking clearly. My actions were automatic. *Get the gun.*

I kept twisting his wrist.

"Drop it!" I yelled.

"No!" David was still in control, and his grip was tight. The more I twisted, the more he held on to the gun.

What I didn't realize was that his finger was lodged against the trigger.

In our struggle, the gun went off.

I didn't feel anything at first. Then a burning sensation in my chest quickly grew to a hot burn that radiated through me and brought me to my knees.

My thoughts returned to our childhood and the traumatic events that brought Trevor and David into our lives. With pain searing through me, I realized another traumatic event was the only way they'd leave our lives for good.

I looked up into my brother's eyes and saw Aaron, which made me smile. *There you are.*

Then everything faded to black.

CHAPTER 38

AARON

"**BRANSON!** No!" My ears rang with a deafening sound, and I couldn't hear. But in my deafness, I scrambled toward my brother, who was kneeling before he fell sideways and hit the floor hard. His body started violently jerking.

I turned him on his back and pressed my hands against his chest that oozed with blood. "Bran, it's me. Stay with me."

His eyes opened and closed.

"Stay with me." I pushed harder against the wound, but blood seeped out of his chest fast—too fast.

"Hold on, Branson. Don't leave me. Please. Branson, stay with me."

My hands shook. *Phone. I need my phone.* With one hand on his chest, I reached behind me toward the desk, grabbed my cell, and glanced at the screen. It was dead. Fucking David.

"Hey, stay with me. I need your phone." I carefully

reached beneath him to his back jeans pocket until his cell was in my hand.

I slid open the emergency screen and punched 911.

"Help." My body shook when the operator answered.

"Nine-one-one, please state—"

"My brother's been shot. Please hurry. We're at 100 State Street, apartment 713." I knew Branson's phone would ping our location to the police because it was an app I'd added to his phone so we could always find him. I left the call open but tossed the phone aside. I didn't want to speak to anyone but my brother.

I pulled him against me and pressed my hands against his chest. I could barely feel his heartbeat.

"Branson, come on, brother. Don't do this. I'm back. He's gone. David's gone."

His eyes flickered open, and I swear he smiled.

"Hey! Stay with me."

But his eyes closed again.

"Branson!" It didn't matter how loud I screamed my brother's name. He never responded.

I didn't know how long it took for the police and paramedics to arrive, only that by then, it was too late.

When they approached us, I refused to let go.

"You don't understand. He's my brother."

"We'll take care of him now," one of the paramedics said.

My tears fell on my brother's cheeks that were cool against me. I tried to keep him warm, but it wasn't working. One of the last questions he asked me deserved an answer.

I gently kissed the side of his head and whispered in his ear. "Do I like you? Of course I like you, Ernie. You're my best friend."

EPILOGUE

AARON

ONE MONTH LATER

THE funeral for my brother was held in Wyoming during the middle of the week. Something about not wanting to ruin a Friday or some shit like that. It was a beautiful service that felt like it would tear me in half. What would I ever do without him?

So many people turned out for Branson. He would've been so surprised. He never realized how many people loved him. My God, he was so loved.

My mom cried, but I'd find her smiling a lot too. Neither Branson nor she deserved any less than my best at the funeral. So when it was my time to speak, I said all the things I wish I'd said more often when my twin brother was alive.

"I want to thank everyone for being here today," I began. I held on to the sides of the podium, hoping it'd keep me from falling.

Little Jack and Carson sat beside my mom in the church. They looked up at me with such hope, like somehow I'd be able to give Branson back to them. But I couldn't, and I knew I was a poor substitute for the brother they loved. The brother we all loved.

"Wow. If Branson could see this," I said to the crowded church and swallowed hard. "Well, he wouldn't believe it." I rubbed my chin, but it didn't stop the trembling.

My mom leaned forward like she was gently pushing me on.

I cleared my throat.

"I was born first, which I never let Branson forget," I said to light laughter. "But Branson did everything first. He walked first, he spoke first, and when he saw the high dive at the swimming pool, he learned to swim the length of the pool so he could be the first to go off the high dive." The memories of our summers swimming were as vivid in my mind as if I were there. "My brother was fearless. Nothing scared him. I may have been born first, but Branson was the leader of our pack."

I lowered my head. Tears fell on the wood grain and slid down just as soon as they landed. It was as if Branson were wiping away my mess—again. I smiled. *Okay, Bran, I'll get it together.*

"So, we all know my brother suffered from mental illness. He owned it. He never shied away from letting people know that he had battled some pretty dark demons. But what many don't know is how many people my little brother saved by his honesty."

My fist came to my mouth, but it didn't stop me from crying. I took a deep breath. *God, get it together. Branson deserves your best.* I brushed my nose in the crook of my arm and didn't care if my suit jacket was stained with snot. I cleared my throat.

"I didn't even know how many people he'd helped until he died. Our house phone hasn't stopped ringing with messages from classmates and guys he met in counseling who credit Branson for helping them stay in the fight." I smiled. "That's so much like him, to help someone, to cheer them on and keep them going. Man, he was a *really* great guy."

I wiped my eyes, but everything was blurry.

"Branson was the strong one. He was the brave one. He knew he had a problem and got the help he needed. I didn't." I shook my head. "I was so afraid of being locked away in a hospital that I hid my symptoms from everyone, including myself. When Branson showed up in Ohio, he knew. He knew I was in worse shape than even I knew. But even when I threatened him, he stayed. He wouldn't leave me." My shoulders shook, and I was losing my hold on the podium. I couldn't imagine a world without Branson.

"He didn't leave until he saw that I'd returned—not my illness but me, his twin brother. He hung on. And then, and I'll never forget this, he smiled." I also smiled at the memory, even though it felt like I couldn't stand. "Branson looked up at me and smiled." I paused. "I'm really going to miss that smile."

I stared at the coffin.

"You know, Branson had that smile, right?" I thought people in the church nodded, but it didn't matter. "His eyes practically disappeared when he smiled. It was funny as hell."

I wiped my nose on the sleeve of my jacket.

"The best thing about being a twin was Branson. He was the best part of me—hell, of both of us. I love him, and I owe him my life." I stared at his coffin like he'd just get up and tell us it was all a joke. Only I knew it wasn't.

"Everything reminds me of my twin brother. Just going through life now, there's something missing, like a puzzle missing its final piece. I feel incomplete without him. And I know I'm not alone." I looked at my mom, little Jack, and Carson. "I know we all feel that way."

I wiped my eyes.

"People have told me that things will get better, but I can't imagine healing from this. What people don't know is what it's like to be a twin. Being a twin creates a bond. Being an identical twin creates a partnership. I lost my best friend." I lowered my head and took a moment while my heart shattered. Then I looked up with tears filling my eyes. "We all lost."

I walked toward his coffin and placed my hand on it. "I love you, brother."

Branson was more than my best friend, he was a part of my soul that disappeared when we lowered him into the ground.

Mornings were the worst. Every time I woke up, it hit me—Branson was gone, and he wasn't coming back. It was like I relived his death every single morning. As if that didn't suck, every time I looked in the mirror and saw his face, it brought more sadness and greater despair.

After we buried my brother, I removed all the mirrors in the treatment facility my mom found for me. I wasn't ready to deal with the reality that the only reflection I would see would be my own and not Branson's. One of the few people who seemed to understand any of this was Hannah.

Sweet Hannah.

She flew to Wyoming and stayed with my family. She visited me daily in the treatment center. She also joined the family support group with my mom, sister, and little brother.

They all had questions, and I wasn't sure my answers satisfied them.

David provided a base, a foundation for me without any judgment. David was there *just* for me. I didn't have to share him with anyone. I was relieved that with medication and counseling, his voice in my head was gone. I no longer felt divided, but I also didn't know what to do next or who I was.

I'd been Branson's twin for as long as I could remember. His absence in my life left a space that nothing and no one could fill—not even Hannah.

She did help me realize that I was not my illness though.

She reminded me that when David was in my head, I was constantly flipping from one thing to the next, starting multiple things at once and maybe only finishing them half the time. It was why I maxed out my credit cards on clothes. I had no impulse control when David spoke, and I was narcissistic as hell. It was a wonder Hannah even stayed. But she had. And so had my family. They didn't blame me for Branson's death, but I did. I knew my twin brother would still be alive if I had been half as brave and courageous as him.

Branson's counselor, Dr. Blaze, visited me and told me that my brother wouldn't want me going through life blaming myself, nor was it a path toward healing. I wanted to heal, but I wasn't sure how that was going to look without my twin.

After a recent family session, my mom returned my cell phone. It had been held by the police in Cleveland while they investigated Branson's death, which was ruled an accidental shooting.

"Damn, you've got a cluttered inbox," Carson said, peering over my shoulder. She sat next to me during family sessions like my new shadow.

"Yeah, I don't have time to read all those emails," I replied while we waited for my mom, who had taken Jack to the restroom.

She laughed. "Bro, I was talking about your voice mail."

I glanced at the voice mail log. A backlog of old messages filled the screen. I scrolled to the top of the page. There was one new message on my phone from Branson. I looked at

Carson, whose eyes filled with tears.

"I'll go check on Mom," she said before she left my room.

My finger shook as I hit Play and held the phone to my ear.

"Hey, bro, I'm coming to Ohio. I'm so excited to see you. It's been too long. I don't care what we do. I'm so proud of you and how far you've come. Ohio seems like it was the right move."

There was a pause in the recording, and for a moment, I thought Branson had hung up. And then his gut-busting laughter filled my ear with the most heartwarming sound in the world. Tears streamed down my face.

"So, bro, I was just thinking about that time we switched classes in the first grade. How about we do that for graduation? I'll finally be able to walk across the stage with honors." He paused again and I held my breath, hoping his message wasn't over.

"Man, I miss you. I can't wait to see what the future holds for you. I know you're going to do great things and make us all proud. See you soon!"

I could barely see the screen of my phone. But I made sure the message wasn't deleted. When the screen faded to black, my reflection surfaced.

"I miss you too, Bran."

The more I stared at the face we shared, the more I realized that I was the only one who could carry on the memory of my brother. If I was going to fulfill his last wish and have that bright future he imagined for me, I had to learn to move on without him. I wasn't sure how that was possible, but I had to try.

I'm going to make you proud.

THE END

ACKNOWLEDGMENTS

Writing heals. When my son Kyle told me he was "hearing voices" during his senior year in high school, I took a scary, uncertain moment in my life and wrote through it. And I wasn't alone—Kyle was beside me the entire time. I loved how Kyle summed up our work at a recent book signing: "We took something bad that happened and made something good out of it." Agreed. Writing is healing.

Writing doesn't happen in a vacuum. By writing through the pain, uncertainty, and fear, Kyle and I were able to heal and move forward. Through writing, the bond I have with my adult son grew even *stronger*.

Writing takes guts. There wasn't anything easy about writing *A Divided Mind* or *The Divided Twin*. Both stories emotionally turned me inside out. And again, I wasn't alone. Kyle was in his senior year of college when we began writing *The Divided Twin*. In between classes and work, he wrote. His journal entries provided the starting point and set the tone. By delving into parts of his past, Kyle allowed me into his pain and straight into his soul. Kyle, I've never been more in awe. You are a natural, beautiful storyteller. Thank you for sharing this journey with me.

My publisher, Becky Johnson, recognized Kyle's contribution and placed his name beside mine on the cover. I don't think I've ever been more honored or proud. Thank you, Becky. Thank you for extending your graciousness, kindness, and professionalism to my son. Thank you for valuing him, his work, and our writing journey. Thank you for putting a face and a story behind mental illness and helping to break the stigma. Thank you, thank you, thank you. xoxo

This story was personal and intense, and no one understood that more than our editor, Kristin Scearce. Thank you for answering my questions—and let's be real, there were a lot, yet you *always* alleviated my concerns. Because at the end of the day, this remains a work of fiction. Kyle and I wanted to write this story to its ultimate apex. We went for broke, and our editor was with us *every* step of the way. So were all our beta readers and extra eyes on this manuscript. Thank you, thank you, thank you.

The Divided Twin was a collaborative process that extended to our beautifully, big blended family. Dylan Gullberg, Max Gullberg, Austin Thomas, Ciara Thomas, and Cooper Pigg—thank you for believing in this as much as we did.

A special thanks to Ciara, our videographer, book trailer creator, and tagline writer. CC, I love you berry, berry, triple berry much—always. Keep making art.

Super Cooper—you are my youngest and the first to read

A Divided Mind. I'll never forget when you phoned to tell me you had finished the book and were mad at me. Clearly, we need more of Jack in every book. I can't wait to see what you think of *The Divided Twin*. I love you so much. You are the highlight to *every* day.

To the man who makes it possible for me to live the life of a writer, Ron Gullberg. My wonderfully bald, sexy man—you are my everything. And I promise *someday* we will have an empty nest. Until that happens, there's no one I'd rather go through parenting, homework, and carpooling with than you. You make everything better—whether it's making the kids mac n'cheese or movie nights in our bedroom, you bring lightness and joy into our lives. The best is yet to come.

And finally to our readers—thank you. Thank you for letting us into your lives and making us feel welcome there.

- Mary & Kyle

ABOUT M. BILLITER

M. Billiter is the alter ego of contemporary, award-winning romance author, Mary Billiter.

After writing more than a dozen love stories, she is exploring the other side. Best known for her emotional honesty, Mary doesn't write about well-adjusted people, but rather the wounds in life.

M. Billiter writes with clarity and raw emotion to explore difficult subjects and issues close to her heart.

TANGLED TREE PUBLISHING

As Hot Tree Publishing's first imprint branch, Tangled Tree Publishing aims to bring darker, twisted, more tangled reads to its readers. Established in 2015, we have seen rousing success as a rising publishing house in the industry motivated by our enthusiasm and keen eye for talent. Driving us is our passion for the written word of all genres, but with Tangled Tree Publishing, we're embarking on a whole new adventure with words of mystery, suspense, crime, and thrillers.

WWW.TANGLEDTREEPUBLISHING.COM

CPSIA information can be obtained
at www.ICGtesting.com
Printed in the USA
FSHW010504130521
81420FS